DISMEMBER THE COOP

Dismember The Coop:
A Charity Anthology Benefitting Alice and Sheryl Cooper's Solid Rock Teen Centers

production are fictitious. No identifica-
tion with actual persons, living or deceased; places; buildings; and products
is intended or should be inferred.

Book Cover by Ash Ericmore

Guillotine Illustration 102930774 © Ilia
Karmilin | Dreamstime.com

First Printing, 2024

ISBN-13: 979-8-8690-3983-5

Dedication

This book is dedicated to Carrie, My Gorgeous Bride, My Love, My Puzzle Piece, and My Person. Yes, that's all the same amazing person. She's always there to encourage me in my pursuits, whether noble or hare-brained, and also to give me a swift boot to the backside when needed. Thank you for always being there for me, Darlin'. I love you.

Table of Contents

Preface

This anthology has been an idea and pet project of mine for some time. Alice Cooper has long been a favorite artist of mine, not just because of the music and lyrics he and his musical partners have generated, but because of his distinctive stage show. Even in <u>his</u> seventies, he's still going as hard as he was in <u>the</u> seventies, albeit in a clean-and-sober and golf-filled way.

But it was his love of horror that led to the idea for this project. Interviews with Alice led me to many great horror films I wouldn't have discovered until much later, such as <u>Evil Dead</u> and many Italian horror classics. Of course, his stage show has always been horror-themed, from the early days with the Alice Cooper group to now. Beheadings, hangings, blood, swords, spiders, you name it.

But part of what makes Alice who he is, at least in my mind, is who he is off the stage. He and Sheryl have been together since the mid-seventies, and she was a key factor in him finally getting clean. When Alice said there were whole recording sessions and tours he doesn't remember, you know it had to be bad. But he made it through to the other side and is still going as strong as ever.

One of the many ways the Coopers have impacted their community is through their Solid Rock Teen Centers, based in the Phoenix, Arizona, area. According to their website, they provide for the "spiritual, economical, physical, and social needs of teens in the community" via non-school hour activities, all free of charge to the teens. So it just made sense to honor Alice and his contributions to not just my life, but the lives of so many, by putting together a horror-themed anthology with all proceeds going to the Solid Rock Teen Centers. If you wish to visit their website to see what services they provide or even contribute a little extra to their cause, you can find them at:

https://www.alicecoopersolidrock.com/

Now, on to the stories in this anthology. When I put out the call for submissions, I was looking for stories inspired by the music of Alice Cooper, not just his solo years, but those with the original Alice Cooper group or even the Hollywood Vampires, his venture with Joe Perry of Aerosmith and Johnny Depp. Specifically, I was looking for stories where the author took a kernel from the song and really ran with it, creating their own supporting characters, backstories, the whole works. I explicitly rejected stories that were basically a song in story format. I wanted something more, something deeper and more creative.

Boy did these authors deliver. Here we have everything from mildly creepy to taboo to humorous, and everything in between. We even have a horror noir story based in the world of the Lace and Whiskey album. Horror, to me, has always been subjective. What may be shocking and a trigger warning to some may be what others seek out. So these stories cover the broad spectrum of horror, really avoiding only excessive violence and sex. Now, it doesn't mean there isn't any, just that it's not over-the-top.

Since we have stories in this anthology written by authors from three countries on two continents, I intentionally tried to retain the style typical for each author's location. So if you recognize/recognise those variances, that's why.

Following each story, I have included the author's inspiration for their story. As you read each offering, I encourage you to look for any Alice-related Easter eggs that might be dropped into the story. There are both overt and subtle ones. It was fun discovering them as I read the stories for the first time, and I anticipate you will get as much en-joyment doing the same.

Finally, I hope you enjoy reading these stories as much as I enjoyed digging into them and putting together this anthology. And please, spread the word about the Solid Rock Teen Cen-

ters, even to those not in the Phoenix area. They are one of the great
programs helping at-risk teens in our
communities.

Bert Edens
Editor
bert@bert-edens.com

"Hallowed Be My Name"
by Paul Lubaczewski

Damnation Witbore rode with barely concealed impatience. It could be said, and often was when he was out of earshot, that he did everything that way. That the man spent his life being consumed by a fire from within. But today there were special circumstances to forgive him. He had been given a sacred task that needed his immediate attention, and just as he had usually found in life, those around him let him down in the end. Was it not the way of sin? To shrink back and appear small so no one saw the great danger it presented, so no one acted with the urgency required? Always people allowed the snake of the devil to vanish into the tall grass because they didn't grab the pitchfork fast enough. Damnation had been pleased to receive his task, and he further warmed to it as he rode. He knew where the devil lay, and the needs of others slowed his pace and held him from his holy deeds.

His wife and children needed to be allowed for, he supposed, but he didn't need to like the pace they forced him to set. The damnable wagon slowed everything; he would have been at his destination long ago without having to wait for the plodding pace of the draft horses. That he would be there without all the tools of his craft, many of which he would need, was totally lost on the man at the moment. Impatience had the upper hand in his mind. He knew not what exactly awaited him ahead, but he would not be going at all if there was no cause. No one calls a witchfinder if there is a dearth of witches.

Madrigal was his destination. The name of the place would, as a matter of course, positively ooze with sin all on its own. But it was more than its name, oh so much more. The idea of the place seemed laughable at first

3

glance, a mere fantasy. A town built and occupied by strolling players? The very concept seemed absurd. What were actors but vagabonds roaming the countryside, thieving from good honest people? No matter how many passion plays they hid it in, thieves and layabouts the lot of them! The less talented they were on stage, the more talent they brought to larceny, and the more talented they were in the footlights, the more likely they were to be in league with the devil himself. The idea of them being able to run a whole town? Insanity! Actor stonemasons? Actor coopers? Madness itself! No, there was more to this, and he'd prove it soon enough. He'd been tasked to.

When good honest citizens had first begun to leave their own towns and cities, not in droves but trickles and drabs, the lords of the land could ignore it. Anyone that would leave the safety of their established cities for that foolishment, well, they could hardly be considered the best and most reliable of citizens, could they? In the beginning, the defections were seen as a net gain overall. If only it had stayed that way, Damnation would have never been summoned.

Once, last year, the town of Hor-landshire had closed its gates to a band of traveling minstrels. The hour had been late, and the lord of the town had opinions on the nature of entertainers. Opinions that weren't far off from Damnation's own, truthfully. Two days later the man had barely had time to make it to the tower to see the retreating cloud of dust that was his eldest son's horse. He had left for Madrigal, and only two of the emissaries the man had sent to the town to plead with the boy to return had bothered to return themselves to tell him his son's answer. It had been a resounding no.

Other towns closed their gates after seeing what had happened in Horlandshire. The results were similar; children, wives, and even a few

6

"chambermaids" leaving. Many of them cursing their lords, masters, and parents as they went. Damnation did not approve of the chambermaids to begin with, not in their relation to those lords. Yet he understood the world and that power allowed you to have those relations outside of marriage. He approved even less of a chambermaid having the audacity to leave the service of a lord who had so welcomed her to his bed.

Word had gotten out soon after, no more gates were closed lest they risk the unspoken punishment of the players. But the lords of this land were no fools, behind closed doors they had hired a witchfinder to root out the source of this evil, the best they could find. They had hired Damnation Witbore.

He put a hand above his eyes and squinted ahead of them. There were the city walls that circled a viper's nest in the distance. There was Madrigal.

"Pull up the wagon, boy," he called behind him.

"What is it father?" he heard over the jangle of tack.

"Tell your mother we camp outside the walls."

There was a pause, probably while the boy squinted ahead himself. "We aren't going into the city, are we?"

"No, you, your mother, and your sister assuredly are not. I value your souls too greatly to risk that. Only I will be entering the devil's den," he replied. Turning and seeing the boy's disappointment, he tried to soften his face, "Now please, tell your mother to make camp, I'll return shortly."

"But father …"

"No buts, Nathaniel! You and your sister are to stay away from that wicked place, and that is final. I assume your mother has the sense to stay away," Damnation snapped at the boy, annoyed at his impertinence.

Damnation rode through the gates of Madrigal proudly, his back as stiff as a board. The guards watched him from their post with bemusement. They looked like guards, but he reminded himself that of course they did, they'd played the role on stage. They were well versed in how to look like guards. How useful either of them would be if they had to actually use those pikes as weapons was anyone's guess.

As he rode down the cobbled streets to present his papers to the town mayor, what struck him first was there was nothing striking to him at all. The town looked and seemed as normal as any other place he'd been in his travels across the land. Maybe even more normal, since by the time Damnation Witbore usually entered a town, there had been so much lamentation and fear spread, a witch was suspected. This town seemed cheerful and clean; people went about their business without a care in the world.

Poor fools. Something must be bewitching them for them to be happy with this unnatural situation. They could not even see the danger they were in in a place like this. They had run away from home to join the merry traveling players like children. And just like so many children before them, they knew not what dangers lay under the powder and dust, what darkness the shadows of the footlights hid from view. He would find it, he would bring it to the surface, and he would have its confession. Then maybe these people would be free to go to their real homes, back to honest cities run by honest lords.

As the banging and hammering in the distance attested, the place was growing.

That had not always been the case. Madrigal had had other names in the past, and those other people who had lived here had left soon enough. It was bad soil that could not grow healthy fruit. The king had almost laughed aloud when the head of the actors approached him and asked if they might try to change the town's fortune. It had only cost the king empty buildings, and considering the ruin the town had always brought to whoever lived there before, maybe it would rid him of no small amount of vagabonds in the process. But it had not failed, no not at all. It not only flourished, it stole, it stole the best and brightest from the towns around it. Every troop of actors who toured now came back larger than it left.

He approached the town hall, appraising the state of the place. An ancient building, built by the first settlers here, it had seen much repair after the last failed attempt to grow apples where only weeds belonged had failed and the town had gone to rot. With freshly painted doors and shutters, flowers growing in pots and on sills, it almost looked cheerful, not a place of town business at all despite the strong stone it was built from.

Damnation handed his reins to a stable hand and walked through the doors with powerful and determined strides. His always barely-contained irritation practically caused his entire form to glow incandescent with rage. He had not expected any of this, and he knew somewhere deep down that what he was being presented with could not be the real picture. Everything around him reeked of falsehood and deception. No group of wastrel actors could have wrought this change on this cursed town. Something else had to be at work, but what exactly was it?

His eyes were drawn away from the door ahead by a commotion in the street. As he watched, a small child stood there in the middle of the cobbles, and it … berated its mother! He had never seen such a thing in his life.

"I told you, mother! We're stopping at the bakery for tarts!" the pint-sized Visigoth bellowed at her.

The poor put-upon woman just shook her head and said, "Yes, Thomas, we'll go there directly."

Damnation gaped at them as the two walked away. If either of his children had ever considered such an action, they'd have been clouted so severely by either him or his wife, they wouldn't be able to see straight for weeks let alone hunger for sweets. Something else that struck him, none of the passersby so much as noted it. Not a single head turned while the miniature tyrant berated the woman who had given birth to him. As if, somehow, this was all normal.

Score one against actors running their own town. No matter how nice it looked on the surface, the rot festered in their hearts. Be that as it may, the wayward nature of its citizens was no concern of Damnation's at this exact moment. He had his credentials to present. He made his way through the door and into the dim room beyond.

16

A man looked up from his desk inside the spacious entrance chamber.

"Yes?"

"Good day, is the mayor available, I am to present my credentials," Damnation said with a firm voice.

The man chuckled and leaned back in his chair, showing his rotund form, "It may surprise you, I suppose, but there's rarely enough real work around here for a mayor to need a clerk. So, I man the desk myself and save the town coffers."

Damnation smiled at that, he appreciated the frugal nature of the statement, "Ah, so good to meet you, my name is Damnation Witbore." He

crossed the distance quickly and handed a series of envelopes to the mayor.

"Well, let us see what we shall see,"
the jowly man said as he took the letters of introduction.

He opened them all with a silver
opener kept on the desktop, slicing
through each of the wax seals before
he perused the top letter. "A witchfinder? Surely we should have no use of
your services in Madrigal!"

Damnation smiled, "Ah, you would
be surprised, many often are. But it
is not any concrete rumor of mischief
or plea from thine citizens that draws
me here. It is the vanishing of some of
the leading children from some of your
neighbors."

"Meaning?" The man's eyes showed keen intelligence as he sharpened his gaze on Damnation.

"Ah, after some of the players who base themselves here had come to call, the heir to the Mayor of Sherbysdale, the eldest daughter of the Mayor of Tideland, and some other towns as well, well they left. Each of them cursed their fathers as they went, I am to understand. Personally, while I think it was a matter of pampered brats running away for perceived freedoms in the life of a player, those mayors suspect otherwise. But regardless of who is correct in the matter, I am to see if I can find them, and to try

19

and convince them to return to home and hearth and duty."

The mayor of Madrigal nodded, "So, am I to aid you in this task?"

Damnation smiled, "No need, sir. I felt that it was better if you knew I was here, rather than having you find out from some other source."

Another nod, "Well, despite what some wags may think, you'll find no need for your main services. I personally don't know the children you speak of; this has become a large town with many comings and goings. It's all I can do to make sure the cobbles get repaired and the guard rotas are approved. But, by all means, look for your wayward heirs, look for all the children who have left their sires to walk off with some pretty lady."

"Thank you, sir, I will do my utmost to conclude matters with discretion," Damnation replied with a thin smile. The man may think he had no satanic rot here, but Damnation was already sure he'd prove otherwise.

"Where will you be staying in town?" the mayor asked. "If I have need of your services while you're here, where should I call?"

"Cities are sinful places; it cannot be helped. To keep myself pure, I never dwell in one. My family and I are setting up camp outside your east gate."

Now that he had discharged the necessary niceties and was returning to his wagon to oversee the setting up of camp, he looked around the city more carefully. Observation was key in his line of work, and he practiced his art whenever time allowed. Witches were masters of deception, the act of hiding in plain sight their bread and butter. The better to work their evil on an unsuspecting populace. One needed a sharp eye to catch them unaware. It was that sharp eye Damnation trained on the town of Madrigal.

Much of the populace of the town dressed like they were in a play. Oh, there was certainly a butcher and a baker, but they didn't look like the real thing. A real butcher or baker was just a man covered in the grime of his task, was tall or short, thin or bulky, but all of them looked overworked and in their belief under-compensated.

Here, the baker was a portly man out of a fairy tale, with what Damnation swore was paint to make his cheeks rosy. The butcher had a stocky muscular build, a perfect build if you'd picture a butcher, but one you rarely saw on the real thing.

Many of the citizens were dressed as if they were lords and ladies at court as they wandered through the streets on their business. A closer look showed that the pale faces so admired as a sign of breeding in royalty took powder to achieve here. The jewels that adorned them were barely cut glass, the white stockings hugging their calves stained and yellowing with sweat. Whores playing at being above their station lined the streets.

On the surface, it looked like a booming town of plenitude, but to Damnation's eye, once again it showed its rot of deception at the core. How could it all work at all? The streets were clean, there was bread coming from the ovens at the baker's, the butcher had sausage in the window. How on earth could a pack of strolling players manage to have this town working so efficiently?

Something unnatural was happening in Madrigal, and Damnation would root it out and destroy it before he left. He worried less about his stated task, about getting the various lords and mayors their whelps back, the more he saw of the place. Once he had tested with fire the evil that lurked here, the children would most likely wander back on their own, and his task would be considered accomplished. He couldn't help a smile. One witch paid well, a town of them ... That amount of money would cause some to consider retirement.

Damnation, on the other hand, loved his work so.

🕷 🕷 🕷

"Did you have good hunting today, my dear?" Clarissa asked timidly as she saw him approach the covered wagon they called home.

"I think I might make enough here to finally buy a house for you, Thomas, and Samantha," Damnation grinned.

"Saints be praised!" she smiled back at him.

🕷 🕷 🕷

Camp had already been made, leaving only dinner to be divvied out as darkness fell. Despite the proximity to such a den of iniquity as Madrigal,

26

the smoke from the city had not drifted this way, and the skies were free
and clear. On a night like this, a man
felt as if he could just reach out and
pluck a star from the heavens and put
it in his pocket. Samantha fell asleep
quickly, her head on her mother's
lap as the woman sewed above her
the inevitable holes in their clothing.
Thomas lay on his back in the grass a
small distance from the fire and stared
into the heavens, entranced as he often was. Damnation approved; a boy
who thought so much on the nature of
heaven would not easily fall victim to
the devil's wiles.

The boy broke the silence, "Father, do you think we'll ever have rooms in a city?"

Damnation's instinct was to scold the boy for his continued impertinence, but considering what he'd seen in Madrigal, the question instead humored him, "Boy, if all goes well here, I plan to buy a little farm. You and your sister won't have to worry about towns and sin again. Clean air and animals to keep will more than make up for it."

They were all silent for a while as this was considered. Damnation felt compelled to add, "Mind, you'll always have these memories of seeing the countryside that other boys won't.

Remember when you get older to be grateful for them."

"Yes, father."

"The hour gets late, time you and your sister were to bed," his wife said as she put down her mending.

Damnation nodded, "I have my bedding here by the fire, I'll see you all come the dawn."

Automatically Damnation knew something was wrong even as the tendrils of consciousness invaded the darkness of sleep. When his eyes snapped open, he could see what it was immediately. The sun, which should have been just now peeking over the horizon, was fleeing the world heading toward dusk.

Damnation scrambled to his feet in a panic. His camp was dead quiet. The fire had long since gone out, and there were no sounds from the wagon. Finally, one of the horses saw him up and whinnied its displeasure with its lack of a morning meal. No, no this was all wrong, he was an early riser, Clarissa earlier still so she could have breakfast mostly made before his eyes even opened. No way would both of them have overslept the day. He had come for the devil, and the devil had mazed them all out in this field!

He rushed to the wagon and threw open the door. Inside there was only one form lying in the bunks, that of his wife. He moved up the steps and inside as quickly as he was able and shook Clarissa roughly.

His wife let out a bleary, "I'll be up to make your breakfast in a moment."

"Breakfast, woman?" he roared. "It's damn nigh time for dinner and bed, and we'll be having it without children tonight."

As the words sank into her bleary thoughts, suddenly Clarissa snapped up and stared wide-eyed around her. "What on earth do you mean, Damnation, where are Thomas and Samantha?"

"Gone. We were mazed by the devil himself. We slept the day away while the monsters stole our children!"

"What will we do?" she demanded, her eyes wide and her voice pleading with him.

"We take God Almighty with us, and we go to get them back," he said. "Now get dressed while I gird for this battle."

She hurried to do as he had said, while he went to get his bag off the back of the wagon. His weaponry was simple, his wheellock; two knives, one silver and one steel; a rapier; a stake of wood; a pin; a Bible; and of course a cross. Most of this equipment was only meant for the capture of a witch, to prove witchcraft took interrogation and in some cases torture, but in the course of their capture, one needed to be prepared for anything. Anything from both the witch and from any family members who sought to protect her. He could only hope it would be enough in an extreme case like this.

Clarissa finally descended the two steps from the wagon, her face a mask of fear and worry. "What should I do?" she asked, her voice strained with tension.

"Go into town like any normal woman. They have more than enough of them there, you should cause no upset by adding to their number. Maybe you'll even have luck today and find them before I do. But in case there's something more sinister at foot, I have prepared myself. The children could have just wandered off, but I doubt it. I think they've captured them to show their power and drive me off. Well, I won't be driven off, do you hear? I will bring God's wrath down upon their heads if I have to bring the whole town to fire!" he declared hotly.

"Do you think it will be safe for me, them being in commune with the devil?" her eyes had gotten wide.

"They present themselves as a normal town, and you are just a woman. They will take no interest in you, especially if you aren't with me when you enter. I'll ride to the far gate, and you can walk to the near one. If neither of us has any luck, we'll meet back here for a late supper and to plan. Agreed?"

She nodded, her face changing from fear to fury. She was nothing if not a timid and dutiful wife normally, but the monsters had stolen her children. "I can but agree, now let us retrieve our children, husband."

It took him some long time, but as Damnation rode to the far gate he paused. There were no guards. Looking past the gate, if he didn't know any better, he'd say the entire town was deserted. There was no noise of a bustling ville to greet him, just an occasional thump or bang off in the distance. He pushed his horse forward onto the cobbles, only to have that become the sole noise to be heard. Had Satan come to take the town along with his children? What must poor Clarissa be thinking walking into something like this?

Suddenly he heard a roar of many voices erupt in the distance, causing him to spur his horse into action. The beast's hooves rang on the cobbles, striking sparks as it went. If the town was celebrating something, he was sure that was where he would find his children. He only hoped it would not be some perversity but just a town festival or the like. The sound had seemed to come from the center of the city, he could only assume that they must have some sort of park or town square located there.

But what if it was something sinister? If he just rode in like a fool, he may strike some down, but the rest were sure to overwhelm him. Damnation paused as he considered it and pulled the reins on his horse. No, his burst of speed had put him close enough to the source of the tumult, he would be better served by some level of decorum now. He dismounted and left the animal tethered to a hitching post. Better to go in on foot to assess the situation before making a fool of himself or worse.

The noise caused by the steady murmur of a crowd reached him, the way it found his ears was curious. Normally a town square or a park had all roads leading to it, but not in Madrigal. For some reason, the only ways forward presented to him were a series of alleys leading toward the center of the town. When he chose one and entered, the closeness of the walls felt claustrophobic, a fear he had never thought he'd suffered from before. Every step felt like agony as he fought down a desire to turn and flee to the open fields surrounding the town.

After forcing himself to move further along, he could hear the crowd roaring its approval at something ahead of him. The sudden burst caused him to freeze in his footsteps. Peering down the alley, he could see the flickering of torches ahead of him already. He was closer than he had thought. Damnation fought down his fear and inched his way closer. He didn't wish to be discovered until he was sure what they were about out there.

A voice cut through the din and the night air. He was sure it was the voice of the mayor who bellowed, "This makes for an auspicious evening, my children! Two new converts to the flock, a sacrifice for our master awaits, and possibly so much more. But first, we should begin our service."

From where he hid in the alley, Damnation could just see out. All the town was gathered around a pit in the center of this park. Past the pit, there was a stake with cordwood stacked against it. There was a person tied to that stake! In the torchlight, he could see their struggles against their bonds, even if he couldn't make out any further details. Could he have been that wrong about them? Would they be doing a witch burning here all on their own? He almost came out of his hiding place, but some inner voice warned him not to.

From where he was, he viewed the mayor holding up a large book waving it around above his head, catching the light. It looked for certain to be the Holy Bible itself. A large and ancient edition, its cover etched in gold leaf, was held aloft for all the townspeople to see. Damnation could scarce believe the words he heard next.

"I curse you, book of the lies of Jehovah and your puny weakling son! I only wish you were with us now so I could crucify you again!" the man declared to an eruption of cheers from the crowd. With that, the mayor walked over to one of the torches and held the book over it until the yellow flame leaped to the pages and they caught fire, after which he threw it behind him like discarded refuse.

"And now that we have rid ourselves of its vile influence, children, who wants to confess their pleasures, make them good, I don't have all night," the man said jovially. "Tell me all your dirty tales of debauchery, I love them all, and more importantly they bring joy to our lord and master. Confess unto me, and there'll be no Hail Marys, only a demand that you do it some more!"

A voice called from the crowd, "I have a grand one, fresh in the moment, and one that all will enjoy. Before we tied her to the stake, we shagged the holy right out of the witchfinder's woman!" The crowd cheered. "And my did she love it as we filled her up, you'd think she'd never seen a pole before from the noises she made! The moment we approached her she bared her breasts to us, and a few moments later we helped her bare the rest!"

A scream cut the air; it was more than a moment before Damnation realized it was his own throat that had let it out. He got control of his voice and stalked forward. The crowd turned and saw him, but instead of fear of being found out, their eyes showed nothing but humor at his antics.

"What in God's name are you doing here!" Damnation bellowed, drawing his sword from his scabbard and his pistol from his belt as he stalked toward the stage. His eyes burned holes in the mayor as he walked, his intense glare so focused on the man who was the ringleader of this unholy church that he spared not a glance for the pit or the stake as he passed them.

"Ah! There you are, witchfinder, I was afraid your faith was too small and you'd run away after giving us your woman as a parting gift." The mayor smiled. The bastard actually smiled.

"Release my wife and my children this instant!" bellowed Damnation, overcome by fury.

The major's smile widened, "Oh yes, the children. Why don't we ask them? Let him pass, my darlings, let him come to the stage to hear the children's verdict."

On to the stage stepped Thomas and Samantha, clean and dressed in new clothes, better than any they had in the cart. Even as they stepped up, Samantha fiddled with what surely must be a wig they had planted on her head. Despite their dress, Damnation's heart almost burst with joy and relief to see them.

"Children, quickly, come down from there. We'll get your mother and flee, but hurry before the mood turns," he said holding his hand toward the stage.

Thomas stared at him, his eyes, which had been sparkling in the torch-light, darkened as he looked at his father. Drawing a great breath he yelled, "You rot! You terrible murdering bastard!"

Samantha looked past Damnation. He followed her gaze to finally see that it was Clarissa who was tied to the stake. She was dirty and naked, she had bruises all over her where they'd used her hard. Satan must have already found her and given her great pleasures in exchange for her soul. Damnation could see the bliss of animal lust in those eyes as they looked back at him. She licked her lips seductively in a way she had never done before, her tongue matching the complexion of her cheeks.

After Samantha was sure he'd seen his wife reduced to this wanton state she screamed, "Whore! Let the rest of her burn hotter than her puss!"

"And it's a damned good one at that! Shame to see her go!" a voice called from the crowd.

Damnation stood there stunned, aghast at all that had befallen him and his family. They had taken everything from him so quickly and with so little effort. Was Satan that strong and God so powerless? It made no sense.

A woman dressed as one of loose virtue came on the stage. She took the hands of both his children, his …

47

children. She smiled at them both and said, "Don't you fear, no more of that life for either of you, poppets. Tomorrow, we'll train you up right."

Enraged, Damnation turned his wheellock toward the mayor, "Unhand them all now, and we will leave this place to you. But I swear by the Almighty, if you do not, I will strike you down where you stand!"

The mayor looked bemused by Damnation's outrage. He chuckled and said, "I would like to see that."

Before he could even consider the loss of a hostage if he shot, Damnation pulled the trigger. He was rewarded by nothing more than a little fizzle from his gun.

"You forget who is lord of the flames, witchfinder. Well, since that won't work, why not join the festivities. We were just getting ready to sacrifice the tramp. Care to light it for us? Or maybe have one last go at her before she burns? At least you know she's wanton, at least five men here will attest to it. Unlike so many of the others, the innocents you condemned to death to get your 23 pounds of payment, she'll have actually communed with sin. So why not get it right this once?"

Before Damnation could say a thing, strong hands seized him. They dragged him in the direction of the pyre laid around Clarissa. He wished he felt more for her now. She had been a good wife all these years, but clearly, she had enjoyed yielding her virtues to these monsters. Clearly, she was dead to him already. He couldn't stand to look at her on his own, so one of them grabbed his head and turned it upright, forcing him to look her right in the face as the first torch flew.

The flames leaped to the sky quickly, the wood must have been well soaked with oil. Before the fire obscured her entirely, she looked at him. Not with fear or pain, no. She looked at him with exultation. She let out one scream into the night as the flames and smoke made her their own.

A throaty scream of "Freedom!"

Damnation's shoulders slumped. In one short day, he was made a defeated and broken man.

The crowd pointed and jeered at him. At last, he forced himself to look up at the mocking figure of the mayor. "Well, I suppose now that I've lost everything, I can leave?"

As the words exited his mouth, an enormous thump came from the pit, followed by another! As Damnation watched in horrified fascination, an enormous gray, taloned hand slammed down on the earth next to the pit with another resounding thump. Followed soon by its mate. A bestial growl echoed in the pit's depths.

"Sorry, but no," the mayor said almost sympathetically. "Your wife was a sacrifice to awaken our master. But he wakes up oh so hungry, I'm afraid. That would be where you come in."

Author Inspiration

Really, that whole <u>Love It to Death</u> album is a collection of stories, wonderfully dark and evil ones. I chose "Hallowed Be My Name," the one I thought I had the most to add to so I could make it my own. But at the same time, if you read the story while listening to the song, it's all in there.

"Going Home"
by D.A. Latham

Clara sat at the kitchen table staring at the envelope in her hand. It was slightly creased with a few dark smudges on the front. The stamp was a playful image of an otter with a snowball. She wasn't sure why she was focusing on these small details. Although it was possibly because she was afraid to open the letter. When she pulled the letter out of her mailbox, the handwriting stopped her in her tracks. There was no return address, but the handwriting was unmistakable. She would know it anywhere.

It had been years since she had seen Ward. Six years to be exact. He had come home from being deployed with the Army. She thought he was home to stay, but he had other plans.

"Baby, this is a good opportunity. I'll be in an elite team of soldiers. The pay is incredible, and it will help us get settled so we can get married and start a family. That's what you always wanted right? A big home and a lot of kids?" he had said, that crooked smile she loved so much flashing.

He knew it would be hard to argue. She wanted to get married before he left, but he had talked her out of it.

They still had time; they were both only 22 at the time.

"You're right," she agreed. "You go, and when you come back, we'll get married and buy a big ol' farmhouse with lots of space for kids."

That night they made love like it was their first time all over again. Two weeks later, he was gone with promises of calling once a month and writing her once a week. During the first month he was gone for this "special elite training," she received a letter once a week like he had promised.

She never did get the call he had promised. Eventually the letters stopped too. There was no one to contact to find out where he was. He had no family except her.

The first few years passed slowly; she cried every night. But life went on, and she got over the man she loved more than anything. She never did start dating again, so maybe she didn't get over him.

Now here she was six years later with a letter in her hand from the man she thought she'd never see again, sitting in the same kitchen where he had promised to come back and marry her. Carefully, she placed the letter on the table and picked up her coffee. Fear kept her from opening it. She didn't want to know what it said.

Clara knew, though, that she needed answers and hoped this letter
contained them. After staring at the
envelope for a while, she picked it up
and opened it. Pulling out the yellow
legal pad paper inside, she unfolded
the letter and began to read.

Dearest Clara,

I'm sure you're surprised to hear
from me. It's only been six years but
feels like a lifetime. I'm not writing to
apologize to you. I think it's too late
for that. What I thought I was getting
into was something completely different.

I know you've changed since I've
been gone. So have I. But my changes

were against my will. When I signed on the dotted line, my life, my mind, and my body became the property of the government. Even now, I hesitate to write this letter to you. I'm afraid it will be found, and I will be punished. I have a friend here who promised to mail this for me. I hope it reaches you.

You can't imagine the horrors I've been through. Experimentation of the cruelest nature. They turned me into a killer, in the most primal of ways. My body is a weapon now. I have no control over the killer inside me. It comes out when it wants.

I don't even think you'd believe me if I told you what I have become. I need to show you.

And this is why I'm writing. I'm coming home. The beast inside me tortures me daily to get to you. I can't promise things won't go badly. But I need to see you. Soon I will escape here, and we will be together again.

Please don't hate what I've become.

Yours,

Ward

Clara stared at the letter, not understanding what she had just read. Was this a threat? There was no date on it, so she didn't know how long ago it had been written. Deep down, she had a feeling she would be seeing Ward soon.

Ward ran through the woods, the wind cooling his overheated skin. He was running away from the tortures of the compound he had escaped from. It wasn't easy, but in the end, it was the scientists' fault he had escaped. They didn't realize by making him a beast he would be compelled to hunt his mate.

He was going home.

Every night since his beast came to him, it clawed at his insides. The only thought that went through his mind was Clara. After six years, his beast could still bring back her smell, the image of her smile, and the sound of her sighs. The way she felt underneath him.

Branches stung as they whipped against his bare skin. Thin lines of blood would trickle down his arms and chest, only to stop moments later. He could heal almost any wound. But it didn't stop the agony of the never-ending pain. His healing was put to the test over and over in the lab.

Ward's mind flashed back to the compound and what he had endured there.

Strapped to a metal table, the men in white coats surrounded him. He tried to yell at them, but he was gagged. He guessed they didn't want to hear his pleas for release, they might just realize what they were doing to a human being. The terror and rage flowing through his body drowned out whatever they were saying. All he knew was there would be pain. There was always pain.

One of the white coats stepped to the table with a scalpel. Ward felt a cool latex-covered hand press against his abdomen. Then the cut. From left to right the scientist cut him open just above his navel. Deeper the blade went until Ward felt it pop through the inner membranes. The scalpel made a clanking sound as it was dropped on the table. That same cool hand reached inside Ward's body and pulled out his intestines. The pain was blinding. Ward's whole body tensed as he screamed through his gag.

The soft plop of his intestines that were dropped onto his stomach made the scientists laugh. They stepped back from the table and waited. Ward's body was covered in sweat, his temperature rising to near a near-fatal level. Every muscle in his body cramped, his back bowed off the table. The sounds coming from him were inhuman. It was like a lion roaring inside his head.

Straining against his bindings, Ward thrashed on the table. His body was on fire. He could hear his bones cracking, feel them breaking apart and reforming inside him. Fingers elongating, nose flattening. The blinding pain in his head was sure to drive him insane as the fissures in his skull widened, changing the shape of his head.

The men in the white coats stepped back a little farther, a bit of fear working its way into their minds. They weren't sure exactly what they had done, but the goal was to create a killing machine. Warily they watched the transformation on the table. When they saw Ward's intestines slowly disappear back inside his abdomen they cheered. A killing machine that can heal itself will make the United States of America unbeatable in any war.

"And there we have it, gentlemen! It worked, the subject has healed from a very grievous wound. The final test has been completed." The doctor smiled at the rest of the team. "Move him back to his cell. But keep him strapped to the table until the rage wears off. Then we celebrate!"

Two of the white coats unlocked the table wheels and pushed it out of the room. Rolling the table down the sterile hallway, they couldn't help but taunt Ward as he lay there panting and groaning. The incision on his abdomen was a faint pink scar now.

"Look at this guy, he's going to make a great pet for the good ol' US of A. Won't you, boy?" The white coats laughed.

Ward remembered the letter he had sent to Clara. He told her he was going home. He needed her. He pulled on the straps that tied down his hands. He felt a little give and continued to pull against his bindings. Ever since the initial experiments they put him through, he had gotten stronger.

Giving one last pull on the straps, Ward put everything he had into ripping free from the restraints. His arms pulled free so fast, the white coats didn't have time to react before he grabbed them both and bashed their heads together. A loud crack echoed through the hallway. As the white coats slumped moaning to the ground,

Ward ripped the gag out of his mouth and undid the bindings on his feet.

Jumping off the table, he grabbed the closest white coat and lifted him off the ground by his neck. Ward's eyes dilated into pinpricks as he smelt the blood dripping from the man's nose. Saliva dripped from Ward's mouth. He was suddenly hungry. He stared the white coat in the eyes as his hot breath washed over the man's face.

Opening his jaws wide, he crunched down on the man's face. Shaking his head back and forth, Ward ripped away the white coat's face and upper lip, leaving a gaping hole that gushed blood. The man gurgled as his own blood flooded his throat. Ward took his other hand and reached into the cavity where the white coat's face used to be and grabbed the tonsils, ripping them free and putting them into his mouth. Ward dropped the white coat as he chewed the lumps of flesh.

Turning to the other man, Ward knelt beside him and flipped him onto his back. Lifting his hand, Ward stared at his fingers with sharp claws at the end. He huffed and plunged those claws deep into the white coat's abdomen. Pushing harder and harder, Ward wrapped his long fingers around the man's intestines and yanked them out.

"You won't heal from that," he growled.

He continued to pull until every inch of the tubular organ was lying on the floor. The man screamed in agony and frantically tried to push them back inside. Ward decided he needed more punishment and lifted the intestines to his mouth. Biting down, he ripped a portion away. The smell of shit joined the coppery odor of blood. The open end of the intestine was leaking feces and Ward shoved it into the man's mouth as far as he could. He stood and walked away with the sound of gagging in his ears.

Escaping from the lab was easier than Ward had thought it would be. He left the halls bloody. Bits of bone, brains, and offal littering the floors. No one was a match for him. He ran out the front door. Not a single alarm went off as he hopped over the fence and took off into the woods.

He was going home.

Time passed and Ward continued to run. He had no idea where he was, but he followed his nose. The farther he ran, the stronger Clara's scent became. Sleep was not necessary, but he did have to eat. As he made his way through woods and small towns, he would hunt. Deer, rabbits, even a fox were easy meals for the monster he had become. The only thing he would leave behind was bones and fur.

Day would turn to night.

Night would turn to day.

He ran.

He fed.

He thought only of Clara.

After several moons, the terrain became familiar. Clara's scent was even stronger. He was close to home. That thought kept him going. A week later Ward found himself crouched behind a tree looking at the house he had once shared with Clara. Her scent carried to him on a breeze, and he growled.

The part of Ward that was still human hesitated to approach the house. Would she be with someone else? That thought had rage pulsing through his body. His claws dug into the tree, ripping away bark.

Would she be able to look at him in this monstrous form? A beast who craved blood and viscera. His physical form was a thing of nightmares. An ugly abomination with no business being alive.

Could she forgive him? He knew not marrying her before he left had let her down. This was all his fault. If he had just stayed with her, they would have the perfect life.

Ward started as a car drove up to the house. It parked out front, and Clara got out. She moved as gracefully as ever as she pulled groceries from the trunk. Just the sight of her made his body react. His heart pounded as he inhaled her scent. Watching her go into the house, he couldn't stop himself from moving closer. Quietly, Ward approached the window at the side of the house. The curtains were open, letting in the sun. He saw Clara in the kitchen unpacking the bags.

His claws clacked against the glass when he placed his palms against the window.

"Clara," he said in the guttural voice that was now his.

She stopped what she was doing and slowly turned around. The jar of spaghetti sauce fell from her hand as she saw the monster at the window. Glass exploded on the floor as she backed up, hitting the counter, her mouth moving in a silent scream. Green eyes wide with terror, she couldn't believe what she was seeing.

Ward punched the window and climbed into the house. He could hear Clara's whimpers, the blood rushing in her veins.

"Clara, it's me. It's Ward," he said, lifting a hand in front of him, his elongated fingers tipped with black claws outstretched.

"W ... W ... Ward??" she squeaked. "You can't be Ward. You're a monster!"

"I sent a letter. I told you I had changed. That I had been changed. This is what I am now. They made me into a killer. I won't hurt you, Clara. I need you."

Ward moved closer to her. He knew she couldn't go anywhere. She was trapped against the counter. The way she looked at him, he knew she couldn't see past the creature he had become. He no longer had smooth tanned skin, his body was covered in coarse brown fur. His face had changed, more angular with sharp teeth and blood-red eyes. Pointed ears. Longer legs and arms.

Drool dripped from his mouth as he put his nose against her neck. Inhaling her scent, he shivered in ecstasy. His mate. The one he needed above all others was standing right in front of him.

"Am I ugly, Clara?" he asked, even though he knew the answer. "Could you still love me like this?"

"I ... I don't even believe you're Ward! Please just go," she wailed.

It felt as if she had slapped him. There would be no salvation in this home where he was supposed to live with the love of his life. Ward dropped to his knees in front of her. He let loose a roar that shook even his soul. What was left of his soul. Without Clara, life, this new life of his, had no meaning.

Anger boiled through his blood. Every cell in his body vibrated with a rage he had never felt before. At that moment, the human part of him retreated and all that was left was the beast. The monster. The thing he had been turned into.

He launched himself up and grabbed Clara by the shoulders. Ripping into her neck with his teeth, he was showered in blood. His body dripping crimson, he feasted on her flesh. Muscles and tendons slid down his throat like ambrosia. His frenzied feeding continued, and blood splattered the walls. Clumps of skin and organs dropped to the floor. He was gorging himself on the person he loved the most.

And he didn't want to stop until there was nothing left.

Chewing on Clara's right arm, he felt a sting in his thigh. He looked down and saw a dart sticking in his leg. He dropped her arm and pulled out the dart, throwing it across the room. A cold tingling sensation took over. His limbs got heavy, and his vision went blurry. Shadowed figures moved into his line of sight. Their voices were gar-bled as a buzzing started in his ears. Ward slumped over, and everything went black.

Eyes slowly opening, Ward blinked against the glaring white light. He tried to look around, but his head wouldn't move. All he could see was metal walls. Cold heavy weight kept his neck, arms, and legs from moving.

"Look who's awake," a deep voice said. A man leaned over him with a smile. "I must say you performed better than expected, Ward. We wanted to make sure the rage could take you over completely. What better way to test that than with the woman you love." The man chuckled. He seemed pleased with himself.

"You were allowed to escape. After reading the letter you wrote to Clara, we knew where you would go. It was the perfect test."

Ward's eyes burned as tears spilled and mixed with the blood caked on his face.

"What a mess you left behind. Had to burn the house down with her body inside to cover it up. Wouldn't do for locals to find that. Poor girl's brains were all over the place!" Again the man laughed.

"Don't you worry, Ward. We'll be taking off soon, and you'll be back where you belong. Isn't it nice to be going home?

Author Inspiration

The song "How You Gonna See Me Now," to me, is about someone who has changed but is wondering if their love will accept them as they are now. They've been apart for a long time and are both different people. Can their love survive? Since one of the lines talks about how the singer doesn't want to be seen as ugly, I wanted to take that in a direction of physical transformation, from human to monster, and will Clara be able to see past Ward's monstrous changes and love him like he loves her.

"Formerly"
by D E McCluskey

A shiver ran through him. It wasn't the first time this had happened. Whenever he heard the sounds, he knew the shivers were coming. They started in his stomach, like a cramp after drinking too much cold water on a hot day. Only these weren't cramps. He'd had them before; he knew where they led.

In an hour he would vomit.

His legs would ache, his stomach would flip, and he would go to bed with bright lights flashing in his head and behind his eyelids.

Formerly …

He didn't know where the word came from, or why he always thought of it, but when the stomach cramps came, that was the earworm that accompanied them.

Formerly …

What did that mean? He didn't have the answers to this, and in an hour he wouldn't care. All he'd care about then was ejecting everything he could from his stomach and making it back to bed without falling over.

'Lee, are you OK?' the shout came from somewhere outside his room. He knew the voice; it was the shrill female sound of someone who cared for him.

Mother? Grandmother? Aunt?

He didn't know anymore. All he cared about now was how he was going to feel in an hour's time.

The noises came from above. Whenever he heard them, they did this to him.

He hated them. They twisted him, wrenched his guts. Horrible mistuned piano notes clanging through his head like rusted church bells, tearing down the walls of his sanity, stripping the wallpaper of his consciousness down to the bare plaster.

They rang out again. Twisted notes, twisted keys. He could feel saliva rushing into his mouth, a recognised precursor to vomiting. Yet the malformed song continued.

A shuffle from somewhere above his room caught his attention. There was someone up there, someone who hated him. He'd concluded a long time ago that whoever it was, hated him, otherwise why would they play that same fucking song all day, every day, knowing what it did to him?

'Lee, are you hearing me?' the female voice shouted again.

It was his mother. He knew that now, could see her face clearly. She would be smiling as she leaned over him, dabbing his head with a wet cloth.

It might have felt good, if only she'd really been there.

'Speak to me, Lee,' she shouted. There was exasperation in her voice, he could hear He wanted to shout to her, he wanted to tell her everything wasn't OK. He wanted to tell her about the boy upstairs, the one playing the fucking piano.

He knew better than to swear.

He visualised the angry, disappointed faces of his parents when he swore.

'Ten-year-olds shouldn't even know the meaning of those words, Lee. Where did you hear them? Who taught you them?'

He wanted to tell them it was the boy in the attic, the one playing the piano incessantly, and so badly.

Formerly ...

There was always a mumble after he heard the word. One he couldn't work out, but knew it was there. A word that hung in the air, between him and ... whoever, or whatever, was whispering to him.

He needed his mother. He opened his mouth to shout for her, but nothing came out. It felt like his breath had been stolen.

He tried again.

Nothing.

He breathed deeply. It was shaky, and it didn't have the desired effect of calming him.

Then the piano rang out again. It was followed by more shuffling. The cramp in his lower stomach twisted again. Strangely, he could taste his mother's mac and cheese. He loved the way she made it. Her secret, one she told him to take to the grave with him, was mustard powder. Not too much to make it obvious, but just a sprinkle. 'To give it an edge,' she'd laugh as she dished it out for him.

'Just the way you liked it,' she'd say.

Lee could never understand why she'd say it in the past tense, but she did, every single time. He didn't understand why, or how, he could taste it now, he hadn't eaten it for a long while. He couldn't remember the last time she had served him her delicious mac and cheese. Worryingly, he couldn't remember the last time he'd eaten anything.

A chord rang out.

He wished he understood music, just so he could correct how wrong that sound was in his head. It was ugly. He imagined an old piano, barely held together, the ivory keys stained yellow with misuse by wrinkled, arthritic fingers pressing them, thrashing at them, bullying them into making vile incoherent sounds.

Maybe they were screams.

He could get behind that thought.

But were they the screams of a mad, demented pianist, or were they the dying cries of the piano, pleading to be put out of its misery?

Both, he thought, as another shudder ripped through him.

'Lee, can you hear me?'

Why didn't she just come up and see him if she were that concerned with his wellbeing?

His legs twitched.

They were restless. He needed to stretch them, to rid himself of the dull ache creeping through his bones, gnawing at the very marrow at the heart of them, but he couldn't. He knew if he moved now, his brain would see it as a rebellion against his body, the dizziness and nausea would gang up on him, and he would be sick.

He hated being sick.

The feeling of dread, as the contents of his stomach rose through his tubes. The bitterness of the bile, the warmth of the frothing saliva. The rush as it ejected from his mouth, while a third of it took the other available route and poured from his nose. The worst part were the chunks left behind when the ejaculation was over. The ones he would have to hike up, and spit, and taste all over again.

He detested being sick, that's why he couldn't stand the noises from above his room.

He closed his eyes, fooling himself into thinking sleep would come. Once again, he couldn't remember the last time he had slept.

He could remember being in school, he didn't know when, but the memory was sharp, valid. Everyone had treated him differently, they looked at him as if they didn't know him. He remembers running away from the familiar, but strangely alien, environment. He remembers crying. His mother comforting him, telling him everything was alright, telling him that things were different now, but it would all be fine. He was home.

It hadn't felt like home.

It hadn't felt like his mother.

He remembered that.

It felt like a hospital, and she was more akin to a nurse. Not a nice, clean hospital that you saw on TV shows, but a grotty place, filled with must, age, and darkness.

It was filled with musty mops and brooms, filled with... holes!

He didn't know what that meant, but the thought of it turned his stomach.

Formerly ...

Holes ... Holes were everywhere. They were in the ceiling, they were in the walls, they were in his skin.

Sitting up in the bed, he only realised it was dark when he opened his
eyes. He didn't remember it getting
dark, but he didn't dwell on that. *Dark
happens,* he thought. *Just like shit.
It's inevitable.*

The curtains to the window were
open and were blowing in the wind,
bringing him to another realisation,
that he was also cold.

Why was his window open? His
mother never allowed him to keep the
window open. He swung his legs out
of bed, and an odd sensation coursed
through him. The room wasn't just
cold, the wind was blowing through
the window, filling the room with a
strong breeze.

This breeze was blowing through him.

It was the strangest sensation he'd ever felt.

He looked down at his naked chest. It was covered in … holes!

His internal organs were pumping, beating, and squeezing behind them. He could see muscle, bone, and veins.

None of this shocked him.

He just allowed the feeling of the wind to envelop him. He wanted to stand, to go to the window. It needed closing, but more than that, it needed looking out of. Something out there was calling to him. He had no idea what it could be, but he needed to see who, or what, it was.

There was also music coming from somewhere out there.

It was sweet. It sounded tinny, overloaded with treble like a harpsi- chord. He chuffed. He was ten years old; how did he know what a harp- sichord sounded like? But he did. It was like something from an old film. It called to him, lulled him towards the window, like a siren of the sea calling to an unsuspecting fisherman, promis- ing him love, succour, the suggestion of eternal life.

The chords of the song were familiar. He knew them from somewhere, but he couldn't think where. It didn't mat- ter. He needed to get to the window, holes in his chest, or no holes in his chest, familiar music or not.

He was feeling braver than he had in a long while.

The wind tickled his insides as he made the short but laborious trip. It was a strange feeling. It hurt, but in a nice way, like how it felt to squeeze a pimple. It stung, but it was satisfying too. His heart was beating up a rock song in his chest. If he looked down, he thought he might see some heavily muscled, long-haired, greased-up man, thrashing about behind a miniature drum kit inside him. But he didn't look, he couldn't. Not only did he *not* want to see his organs inside him, but his need to see who was calling to him was too strong.

The night was bright, almost too bright. The moon was shining brightly in the sky, casting its silver tint as far as the eye could see. He had an odd urge to dance, up there in the attic, and he felt his feet tapping along with the sweet melody in the air.

Covering his eyes from the glare of the moon, he could make out a grave-yard outside. He'd never noticed it before. He'd always thought it was just fields, open fields where he used to run and play, living his youth.

Before the holes, before the wrin-kles.

He was a young boy in an old man's body.

The graveyard, *formerly* his playground, looked very different.

There was a man out there. Or was it a boy? He couldn't tell, his eyes were not what they once were. He was standing before an open grave, waving, swaying in time with the music. He could see that whoever it was had dressed for the occasion, yet his clothes were shabby. They were old and motheaten, like he'd taken them from a corpse. He wore a dark smoking jacket with a silk shirt underneath.

If fact, the man resembled a corpse. One who had just climbed out of its grave to dance. To entice him over into the next life, like a groovy skeleton from an animated film he remembered watching, not that long ago.

There was something about this man he recognised.

He's my father! The thought came from nowhere. It scared him.

He's my son! This thought didn't scare him as much as the first, but it did confuse him.

His father wasn't dead.

He had no children. He was only ten years old for God's sake.

'Formerly ...' the man shouted.

The word hit him like a freight train.

'What?' he shouted in return.

'Formerly ...' the man shouted again. There was laughter in his voice as he cavorted around the graveyard, waving his arms in the air like a lunatic, kicking his legs high.

'Be careful,' Lee shouted, reaching out the window, attempting to warn the man that he was dangerously close to the edge of an open grave.

The man either didn't hear him or didn't heed his warning, as he danced too close to the edge, and the earth beneath him crumbled. He watched it happen, as if he were down there with him, between the tombstones.

With a comical wave of his arms, the strange man in the musty dinner jacket disappeared into a hole.

The hole.

His Hole …

Lee jerked awake.

The horrible music was still banging around inside his head, still scratching, filling him with nasty feelings that ran the length of his body.

'Mom,' he whispered, amazed that the words had come from his dry mouth.

'Lee, is that you sweety?' his mother shouted up to him again from some-where else. She sounded closer, like maybe she was in the hall, as opposed to the kitchen where she had been be-fore. He tried to envision the hallway but couldn't.

All he could see in his mind's eye was the outside of a house in the night. There was a window three stories up. It looked like an attic. Someone was waving to him from that window, someone he knew, someone he recognised.

It looked like he had ...

Holes!

Lee had holes in his memory.

Why can't I remember what the kitchen looks like?

The music in his head clawed at his brain, ripping away his grey matter. The vomiting would begin any minute, he could already feel it churning in his stomach.

'Holes,' he whispered.

'What was that sweetheart?' his mother shouted.

'I said ... holes!' It hurt him to shout this reply, and he felt goosebumps rise on his skin.

In return, he received silence.

Even the sounds from outside, cars passing, birds singing, dimmed. A sharp agony took hold of him, erupting from the centre of his head.

The boy waving in the window, he thought. *He had holes in his body, in his head. What had he said the name of the song was? Formerly?*

'Formerly ...' he whispered.

'Yes,' his mother shouted. 'That's right. Formerly!'

Nothing was making any sense to him.

He wracked his ten-year-old brain, trying to remember what that word meant. All he could think of was a man in a ruined smoking ...

Fuck! he thought, wincing at the cuss word. He'd get into trouble for that. The boy in the window, the one with the holes, he was formally dressed. He wore a musty old smoking jacket and a silk shirt.

No, he was naked.

His brain was playing tricks on him. The boy had been naked at the window, he knew that, because he could see the holes in him.

The agony from the centre of his brain struck again. He screamed. This time there was noise.

Why had he not been sick?

'Is it working?' his mother shouted. Now she sounded on the stairs, just outside his room.

Is what working?

He could see the stairs. He knew what they looked like, and he could see the hallway at the bottom of it.

Someone was looking up.

It was a boy. He was young, but ancient at the same time. His skin was wrinkled, flabby, old. There was a hole in the centre of his head. Lee could see his exposed brain. He was bald, his mouth was hanging open, and Lee could tell the child was screaming, only he wasn't. In his hands, hands that were almost not there, he held a silver tray. On the tray was a comically large key.

Instinctively, he knew it was a key to a heavy wooden door.

It was a door he'd seen before.

Was it in another life, or had it been earlier today?

It could just have easily been a thousand years ago.

He hadn't wanted to go through the door. This he could remember, but strong hands had forced him.

The withered old man, who was really nothing more than a child offered the tray to him. The key rattled on the metal surface. He opened his mouth to say something, but a chord, a twisted cacophony of nonsense from the yellow-stained keys of a harpsichord rang out instead.

It echoed through his brain, as horrible images ran through his head.

He watched, as a disenfranchised hand reached out to the freak with the silver tray. He knew it was his own hand, he knew it was his arm extending towards the dithering old child. As his fingers stretched, reaching for the brass key, the harpsichord got louder.

'Is it working?' his mother shouted again.

111

He wanted to ask her if what was working, but he couldn't speak, he could barely think.

This was the key to the heavy door, the one he had been bundled into and strapped to the bed …

He touched it. The metal was cold, and it bit into his fingers. He gasped, withdrawing his hand.

The music stopped.

His vision tunnelled. All he could see was the remnants of a human before him. A man/child looking at him with eyes that were milky white. He had holes in his body that were big enough to fit a fist through. He should have been leaking. Body parts, organs should have been seeping through the holes, but they didn't. Even as the stranger shook, like jelly in an earthquake, nothing seeped from him. The boy/man was difficult to see, the holes were causing trypophobia, and the nausea was making an unwelcome return.

'Lee,' the man/child spoke. It was more of a whisper, a scratch.

'What?' he replied.

'Lee,' the ancient child repeated.

'What?' Lee asked again, a little louder in case the, he didn't know what to call it, hadn't heard him.

'I'm Lee,' it whispered, his voice as withered as his body.

'I'm Lee too,' Lee replied, feeling somewhat confused at this coincidence.

'You ...'

'Yes, me!'

The man/child shook his head. Lee watched his brain move independently through the holes. 'You ... need ... to ... get ... away!' he stuttered. Then, with a violence Lee wouldn't have thought the man/child to possess, he thrust the silver tray at him.

The key dropped to the floor. It fell in slow motion, and they both watched it fall.

'Formerly ...' he whispered, before the holes in his body expanded. They became so wide and so deep, that the thing that had identified himself as Lee ceased to exist.

Shaken, he tore his gaze away from the nightmare before him and looked at the key on the stairs ...

'Lee, can you hear me?' his mother shouted again. 'Answer me.'

She sounded annoyed, angry.

The key on the floor was calling to him, much like the man in his dream, the one in the attic, while he danced in the cemetery.

That wasn't my dream, he thought. *It was someone else's ... It was Lee's!*

'Lee, can you hear me?'

The music was no longer screeching, it was no longer a mess of notes that didn't belong together.

It was a melody.

It was beautiful.

He never knew music, or had never known it before anyway, but the names of the chords came to him. C minor, then G, then G sharp, F, B flat, D sharp, G with an added seventh.

None of it made any sense to him, except that it did.

It flowed through him, he could feel it in his hair, it was in his teeth, it flowed from his fingertips, from every single pore in his skin. The music was his.

The song was called … Formerly!

Humming along, lost in the cadence and rhythm, he picked up the key.

He was in a class. In his arms was the large wooden body of a classical guitar. Before him, on a music stand, was a song. It was one he'd written.

He recognised the chord pattern.

He'd heard this song before, in his head, for what felt like a million years.

It was his song!

The scene flashed forward, he was in a cafeteria, in school. He knew everyone, everyone knew him.

His clothes were old-fashioned. Perhaps a fashion from ten years earlier. The cars parked in the lot outside the window were older too. He looked at the registration plates, none of them were recent.

Next, he was walking home.

Then without warning he couldn't see. His hands were bound, and something was in his mouth, stopping him from screaming.

Without any further warning, he was being pushed through a door at the end of a narrow staircase. The door was wooden, and in the old-fashioned lock there was a comically large metal key.

The pain was real. It was searing, screaming agony.

Only it wasn't him who was hurting, it was someone else; another boy lying naked on a table next to him. He knew this boy's name was Lee.

This boy had holes in his body. Tubes were attached to the holes. Dark liquid pumped through them.

'Lie still, Lee,' the female voice snapped.

The boy with the holes turned to look at him. As he moved it became obvious that his skin was older than the boy. It was used, flabby, wrinkled. His body was contorted, disfigured, old before his time.

'I'm Lee,' he whispered. His eyes were older than they should have been. 'The third Lee,' he whispered, tears filling up his rheumy, white eyes. 'Former Lee!' He attempted a smile, but it was hideous in its melancholy.

Lee felt a pinch in his skin.

An alien hand, a woman's hand, the hand of someone he didn't know had been in the room. She was holding a small, surgical knife.

He screamed as agony filled his head.

The hole in his head!

An odd sensation wracked through him as something was inserted into the hole. The pain changed. It was something more than agony. It tran-scended torture. It was a parody of music.

He knew the chords, he had written them, composed them from his own imagination, but whoever was playing now didn't know how to form them correctly.

A peace filled him as he drifted into oblivion. His only discomfort was a slight cramp, twisting in his stomach, the spasms were in perfect time with the ugly chords.

'Hurry up, Lee,' his mother shouted as she ushered him up the stairs, towards the attic. She turned the metal key in the lock and pushed the heavy door.

He had never been up here before. He'd been warned never to play up here. Old habits die hard, and he was reluctant to enter. 'What are we doing up here, mom?' he asked, catching his breath. The stairs had been steeper than he'd imagined.

'It's a surprise, for your fifteenth birthday,' she replied, opening the door. 'It's your coming-of-age present.' She swung the heavy door open, revealing a dark room beyond. She ushered him inside and, closing the door behind her, turned on the lights.

What he saw terrified him.

There were four boys, each progressively younger than the last, lying on metal tables.

When the light fully illuminated the room, they all turned their heads at once, their milky eyes regarding him. Their gazes were devoid of emotion. The boy on the first table looked no older than three. His body was aged, wrinkled, and dry.

The second was a little older, but only by a few years.

And the next, and the next.

Each body was dressed in clothes that looked like they had been pulled from a corpse. Musty, dark blue velvet jackets, with motheaten shirts beneath them.

They looked dead, but he knew they weren't.

'What ...'

'These are your brothers, Lee. Each of them, a Lee, in their own right. All of them, former Lees.'

'Why? Mom ...'

'My baby was dying,' his mother whispered, as she slipped into a white coat. 'I needed to prolong his life, so I took his essence and put it into these other boys. The only problem I have is that they don't seem to be able to survive longer than a few years.'

Lee looked at his mother and the man behind her, who he'd thought of as his father. 'What's ...'

The man smiled at him. It was a friendly smile, filled with warmth and love, but there was something else behind it. Was it weariness? Madness? Lee didn't know, he didn't want to know.

'You're deteriorating, Lee,' the man he thought of as his father continued.

'That's why the kids in school look at you funny. You're old before your time.' He smiled again. 'We need a new Lee. A Lee who can carry our baby into adulthood.' He sighed. There was genuine sadness in the rush of air. 'That's just not you, son.'

Before he could run, before he could try to make his escape from this hellish room, from his decrepit brothers, the vile clones, his mother pushed something sharp into his neck. The other Lee Warmers watched as his vision doubled, as a cacophony of vile, mistuned, unstructured music filled his head.

He saw a house. It was dark. There was a large full moon hanging in a cloudless sky. There was a window on the third floor, it was the only one that was illuminated. From out of this window four people waved to him, each of them covered in holes.

He looked at himself, his smoking jacket was torn, musty, old.

His brothers continued to wave.

He wondered what they thought of him.

He didn't want to be one of them. He didn't want to be another former Lee Warmer!

Author Inspiration

My inspiration for this story is that my all-time favourite Alice album is <u>DaDa</u> … It's so creepy, and just so GOOD. "Former Lee Warmer" is just one of the songs that scream ALICE COOPER to me. It is creepy, claustrophobic, and just madness. It conjures 1970s horror to me, where you just don't quite know what is happening, you just know that it's horrible, and you shouldn't be enjoying it … but you are. That is what I have tried to get across in my story …

"Carnival Ride"
by L. V. Gaudet

Steeeven," an unseen voice hisses in the silent darkness, the name hoarse, drawn out. The sound brings a new chill to his flesh, digging deeper than the icy fingers of the cool air.

The barest of pinpricks above provide no light, dark clouds streaking across the sky hiding most of the stars.

A distant sound invades the muffled silence, radiating its own ghostly glow of weak light. Soft at first, growing closer, intensifying, invading, swallowing the world in a cacophony. Off-key, jangling carnival music fills the air with clashing songs, muted garishly dancing and flashing lights, and the hiss of steam, its mist soaking into the night.

Swallowing the little boy standing alone staring up with wide frightened eyes, his mouth a small stunned oh.

He is frozen in place. Wants to run. He can only squeeze his eyes shut and try not to hear the overwhelming racket drowning him.

He opens his eyes again. Chill, hard metal presses against his back and buttocks. A hard, double-iron bar is clamped down only inches above his thighs. His small fists grip another bar before him.

The ground is far below, the lights and sounds so far down now. How?

All he can do is stare mutely.

With a rough shuddering clank, the ride car shivers and lurches, throwing him forward against the bar.

Metal screeches, and the music below plays louder, faster, the lights flashing harder.

It jostles again, clanks, and descends on a trembling arm that feels like it will let go, dropping him and the car to his death.

Steven wants to cry out, clamber free, and escape. There is nowhere to go. The approaching ground is a relief. It will stop. He can get off.

The chair swings and rocks back and forth when it reaches the bottom, changes direction, and begins its rough ascent.

He reaches out, fingers splayed, as if he could grab the earth and pull it back, mouthing the cry silently, "No!"

The ride goes up and up, reaches its climax, and begins the descent again, steadily, shuddering and clanging uneasily, up and down and up again.

This is wrong. The midway closed years ago. He can't be here.

The memory of this same carnival flashes before him, newer and less terrifying, but still a scary place for a little boy. Especially the fun house with its unending mirrors, windows into endless new worlds, and its inevitable impossibility of being escaped. The fun house always scared him.

Jogging through the winding forbidden paths between rides to move faster around the crowds filling the midway. Clanging bells and tooting horns braying to the zoop whirl of spinning prize wheels and carnies crying out their games. Footsteps before and behind, turning to grin at his friends as they race to the next ride or game of skill they wanted to try.

Mostly they eagerly watch others thrill in the entertainment with large grins and wide eyes, wishing they had money, eyes scanning the ground for any lost tickets or coins.

Steven's wide eyes and grin are sickly. The paint fades and metal stains with rust, rides growing creaky and clanking, lights dimming with age.

He is in the ride car again, going forever up and down and up. The carnival below is ruined, deserted, and dark. His friends have all gone home. The garish lights a flashing memory, fading with the off-key hooting notes of the calliope music and whizzing bell-ringing chaotic clamor of the midway. A small boy.

Tears burn his eyes, and his breath catches in his throat. He can't breathe.

He wants to cry. Mommy. I want out of here.

Looking down, the world is wrong. It's not the abandoned carnival. A world of darkness, cloying silence, the music and lights gone but echoing in his head.

Below in a single pool of light are scattered toys of his past, broken.

"Did I do that? I don't think I did. Did I? I must have."

He looks at his wretched hands, the hands that must have smashed and torn apart those toys. Who else would have? Thinking, how could a small boy's hands do such damage?

His hands are thick and long fin-
gered. The hands of a man. He is a
man.

"No, I'm a little boy." His voice is still
that of a small boy.

Fear slices through him, filling him,
an icy knife that would shred him. Fear
of what? Being a man or a boy?

"I'm a man. No, I want to be a little
boy for a while. I don't want to go
back."

"We have to go back." It is a man's
voice that answers. "Our mother will
be calling. She always does."

He blinks back the tears streaming
down his cheeks. He is a small boy
again.

Rain starts to fall, soaking him, its steady hiss drowning out the fading echo of music in his head.

"Steeeven," an unseen voice whispering in the silent darkness. It is a woman's voice. Soft and sad. The sound brings a new chill to his flesh, digging deeper than the icy fingers of the cool air. "Steven, please. Come home."

Cold. Darkness. A clammy dampness that clings to the skin.

He blinks. Tries to blink. Gummy lids glued shut. His eyes are grainy and sore.

The world is fuzzy through his slit-ted eyes. He rubs them and can blink them open wider, but the world still does not want to come back.

He feels wretched. A soul-wearying heaviness.

The world swims unsteadily into blurry focus. The partially-decorated, half-finished basement furnished with worn throw-away furniture. The sallow light of a table lamp, its shade askew, pushes the shadows to the edges of his vision.

His hands are gripping the arms of an old easy chair, fingers indenting with their tight clutch. The hands of a man.

A low whining rumbling moan breaks the silence. His empty stomach, hollow, letting its unhappiness be known.

He is so hungry. His mouth is so dry, his lips feel cracked and his tongue pasty and swollen.

It takes effort to make his fingers release their grip and pry them from the chair.

He looks around, confused, unable to pull a full thought together in the grogginess still clinging to him.

"H-how did I get here? Did I sleep-walk?"

He feels small. A little boy inside the man's body he cannot fill.

His wife comes to his mind, alone in their bed upstairs. Is she sad? Is she wondering where he is? Did she whisper his name in the darkness, soft and sorrowful?

Getting unsteadily to his feet, he wavers a moment, then lurches forward, and for a moment it feels like the mechanical lurch reminiscent of an old clunking and creaking carnival ride chair.

Steven stumbles forward to go find his wife then stops. He focuses to see, fuzzy darkness still pressing against the edges of his vision, against the edges of his thoughts.

On the floor is a crimson drop. And another. He looks beyond them, and there is another, then more.

"What?"

The drops go up the stairs, the house above silent and dark.

He follows the trail up the stairs and out the back door into the night, cool dewy grass wet against his bare feet. Across the backyard, one corner touches the tip of a triangle of undeveloped land thick with weeds and tall grass trying unsuccessfully to push out the trees and bushes that were there before.

It is somehow darker in there, still the pale round moon above gives enough light to follow the crimson trail.

Steven does not feel the rough stalks and thistles crunching under his feet as he enters the untamed ground. A sense of déjà vu teases, opens its hideous maw, and swallows him like a silent cacophony of glaring flash- ing lights and demented organ music swaddles a small, frightened child with numbing finality.

He looks down at his hands. Clarity washes over him, making him stagger. His hands are wet, soaked in crimson, dripping.

He sees now the red-smeared arms of the easy chair in the basement, the smudge pressed up the wall from his bloodied elbow, the wet crimson slowly drying on the brass back doorknob next to red ruined fingers on the edge of the door.

And he feels like a man, looming, lurching, darkness-filled. Powerful. The horrid memory that won't come is a vague sense of badness pressing against him.

Steven stares ahead though the bushes and trees. The imperfect path lit by the moon, clawed shadows of branches on both sides reaching for its center appear as the clawed crooked hands of minions of Hell reaching to grasp him, to tear him apart, and drag him down to the netherworld.

He staggers forward, cringing away from the nearer reaching shadows, almost feeling those claws inches from digging into his flesh. Stumbling on, crimson drops on the ground leading him forward, hands wet, feet numb to the cold, dewy stinging vegetation and sharp rocks of the path. The tall grass and weeds pressing against the trail, encroaching and trying to wipe it away, whisper sinister secrets he can't quite make out as they brush against him.

Then around a curve there is almost a clearing. A widening, grass and weeds trampled down, and something discarded there, carelessly tossed trash of clothing. But it is not clothing. It wears it, dirtied, soiled.

Stumbling forward, he falls to his knees next to it. To her.

A sob chokes out from him, almost a tormented, barked laugh of wretched sorrow.

"No," he moans. "I don't want you gone."

He closes his eyes to shut it out, covering them with his bloodied hands.

"I don't want to be here."

"Steeeven," her sorrowful voice whispers softly in his head.

"Go away," he begs in a hoarse whisper. "You barely lived. You have years more."

He pulls his hands away, leaving red smears on his face, and stares up at the night sky.

"Why did you leave me?"

"Steeeven," her voice cries in his head. Screams echo there, overlapping in their own wretched, ugly carnival song.

He covers his ears, still staring up.

"Stop screaming! This isn't real. You aren't real. Please, this is a dream."

His arms drop to his sides, and he looks down at her motionless form, waxlike pale face half covered by the hair fallen across it. The screams in his head have faded.

"You know I don't like it when you cry. It hurts me." He pounds his chest. "It cuts me, here."

He closes his eyes tight again, as if that could make it all go away.

"Steeeven." The screams, far away, echo in his head, whispering in the night air surrounding him, crying out his name again and again, begging and pleading, an icy sigh wailing weakly in pain.

Looking down at her, he tenderly draws the hair back from her face. He is filled with the emptiness of loss, the ghostly whisper of her essence fading away from him.

"I-I feel you dying. I felt you leave me. I don't want to feel that."

He reaches to gently close her eyes, but they do not stay closed. He closes them again, and again they do not stay.

"If that's the way God wants it."

He tries again, getting frustrated with those eyes staring emptily at him.

"If it's God's plan to take you now."

His frustration grows with another attempt to close them. He cannot stand her watching him.

"Stop looking at me," he breathes at her lifeless form.

Steven brightens with an idea.

Digging in his jeans pocket, he finds coins and pulls them out, dropping some on the ground.

"Pennies for your eyes."

Closing them again, he places a penny on one, then a nickel on the other, to weigh them down, hold them in place, a mismatched offering to

Charon for the ferry crossing the river Acheron.

He closes his own eyes again, uneasily settled, with a ragged sigh.

"It will go away now."

The cries won't stop haunting, barely there, teasing and tormenting at the edges of his consciousness. Icy wails crying out his name. Begging and pleading.

"No. It's not real. It's a dream. I-I think someone is calling me. Wake up, Steven, wake up. I don't want to be here."

He looks around.

"Are you calling me? Trying to wake me? Mommy?" His voice is small, imitating a child's. "The door. You are outside the door."

Steven looks around, bewildered, but the door is only the night world beyond the little clearing outside.

The voice keeps calling out his name.

"What? What do you want with me? Why are you calling me?" he screams into the night.

Running through the darkness back to the house, Steven bursts in through the back door. Stumbling through the house, leaving a trail of dirt and traces of leaves, he searches for her.

"Where are you?"

It is night. She must be in bed. He lumbers to the bedroom. The bed is in disarray and empty.

Steven bumps against the dresser and turns. A frightful visage stares back at him in the mirror, made all the more terrible by the shadows of the darkened room.

"Who is that? It's not me."

He leans in, staring harder. The face is dirty with flecks of grime and blood. Nails dug in and scratched down one cheek, weeping a drying trickle of blood from the ruined flesh. A purplish bruise is growing below one eye. The hair is as wildly manic as the eyes glaring back at him, red-rimmed and bloodshot.

"Is that me? But I'm just a boy. I don't want that to be me. No, that's not me."

Fumbling around on the dresser, he finds his wife's makeup.

He puts it on, smearing foundation across his face, trying to conceal the horror staring back at him.

It is not enough. Tossing it down on the dresser, he lurches from the room.

In the basement he rummages in boxes, finding the drying and cracked old stage makeup bought cheap when last they dressed for a Halloween party years ago.

Sobbing, he digs his finger into one of the flat palettes and smears it across his face as he scoops them up with the other hand and brings them upstairs.

Steven staggers to the fridge and takes a beer, gripping it against his ribs with his elbow to crank off the cap with a wretched sorrow-filled twist. He swallows a long draught as he stumbles away, blinded by his self-loathing misery. The chilled liquid wets his parched mouth and slices icily down to his belly in painful release from his thirst.

Returning to the bedroom, he smears on more makeup at the mirror, staring into his bloodshot eyes. Painting his face like one of the carnival clowns that always brought a sharp clamp of fear gripping his stomach as a child.

The face could be cruel or terrifyingly happy. A demented visage out of a horror story.

It makes him feel safer. It is something to hide behind.

A distant sound invades the muffled silence, radiating its own ghostly glow of weak light. Soft at first, growing closer, intensifying, invading, swallowing the world in a cacophony. Off-key hooting notes of calliope music fills the air with clashing songs, muted garishly dancing and flashing lights, and the hiss of steam, its mist soaking into the night.

The overwhelming noise drowns him. Swallows him. He is a little boy standing alone, staring up with wide frightened eyes, his mouth a small stunned oh, face painted in terrifying clown makeup.

He can hear and feel the crowds filling the midway, but there is no one there. Clanging bells and tooting horns braying to the zoop whirl of spinning prize wheels and carnies crying out their games. Footsteps before and behind. He turns to grin at his friends, but they are all gone.

When the morning dawn invades the room, his wits come back, but only enough.

Wiping off the makeup, he strips the muddied bloody clothes to dress in something fresh and goes to work.

Coming home again, Steven grabs his beer from the fridge and goes back to the bedroom to paint his face anew. Taking him back to the carnival, that place he despises, that he both feared and reveled in as a child.

"Steven." His mother calling from far away.

Each day is the same. He goes to work and comes home. Sobbing in his beer as he paints on a face that might be cruel or happy. Dark circles have replaced the bruise under his eye, darkening, blacker and bluer.

Each night he escapes to that frightful midway, losing himself in alcohol and self-pity.

When he sleeps, if he sleeps, she whispers to him.

"Steven, come home."

But Steven doesn't come home. He stays out smoking and drinking. When he does come home, he slaps his hand on the table, demanding his meal while she scrambles to please him. He lies to her face about where he has been, angered by his guilt, knowing she has cried alone at night again.

He slaps her, throws the food across the room, bellowing at her to feed him something better, shoving her to the floor as she begs and pleads.

"Clean up this mess," he spits at her.

On her knees staring up at him, face tear-streaked and bruised with blackened eyes. The new bruise already beginning to show its face, taunting him.

"Steven, look at me. Look at what you are doing to me. I can't buy food if you won't give me money for it."

"Shut up," he snarls, and he paints on his makeup again.

"Steeeven," the off-key organ music calls out his name. Clunking clanging metal banging quietly. The whispered sigh of faraway clanging bells and tooting horns braying to the zoop whirl of spinning prize wheels and carnies crying out their games. Crowds of shuffling feet.

Voices echo from down the hall.

A white antiseptic room. The remnants of scrawled drawings are smudged on the walls where someone tried to scrub them off, rats and spiders, and black blood dripping from staring black eyes.

Steven lying in bed, grins. His bat and rubber ball on the bed next to him.

He is a little boy, but he is a man.

"I'm just a little man, a wind-up toy. I get up when they tell me and lie down when they want," he sings softly. "Mommy doesn't want a wind-up toy instead of a boy, and daddy won't talk about me."

Something dark scurries on the floor. He knows it is there, sees it without having to look. It scurries out under the door, spider legs dancing, their hair tingling, fangs drooling, hunting.

"My little friend, you are free to crawl under the door. You all are, to come and go," he sings.

Steven holds a hand before his eyes, staring with wonder.

"Look, my fingers aren't shaking." He stops singing.

He turns his head to stare at the door. Footsteps are approaching. He is alone in the bed, bat and ball gone.

The door opens. There is no one there.

"They come at night," his little boy voice says. "Every night. Do you see them? I'm so tired."

He closes his eyes.

"Steeeven," the carnival music calls out his name. Clunking clanging metal banging quietly. The whispered sigh of faraway clanging bells and tooting horns braying to the zoop whirl of spinning prize wheels and carnies crying out their games. Crowds of shuffling feet.

"Mommy," Steven asks, the little boy looking up. "Where's daddy?"

"Steeeven," an unseen voice hisses, the name hoarse, drawn out.

"Mommy, I will give her back her playthings if you let me out of here. Even the ones I took. She was just four."

"Mommy, there is a man choking there. I can hear sirens."

The wail of sirens sound like they are calling out his name and fade away.

A distant sound invades the muffled silence, radiating its own ghostly glow of weak light. Soft at first, growing

closer, intensifying, invading, swallowing the world in a cacophony. Off-key
hooting notes of organ music fills the
air with clashing songs, muted garishly
dancing and flashing lights, and the
hiss of steam, its mist soaking into the
night, filling the air with clouds.

Swallowing the little boy standing
alone staring up with wide frightened
eyes, his mouth a small stunned oh.
He is frozen in place. Wants to run. He
can only squeeze his eyes shut and try
not to hear the overwhelming racket
drowning him.

He opens his eyes again. Chill, hard
metal presses against his back and
buttocks. A hard double-iron bar is
clamped down only inches above his

thighs. His small fists grip another bar before him.

The ground is far below, the lights and sounds so far down now. How?

With a rough shuddering clank, the ride car shivers and lurches, throwing him forward against the bar. Metal screeches, and the music below plays louder, faster, the lights flashing harder.

It jostles again, clanks, and descends on a trembling arm that feels it will let go, dropping him and the car to his death. The chair swings and rocks back and forth when it reaches the bottom, changes direction, and begins its rough ascent.

Steven wants to cry out, clamber free, and escape. There is nowhere to go.

He turns, and there is a man in a strange suit and too-tall top hat sitting next to him.

"The carnival is closed, boy. The sideshows are all shut down. They've run us out of town."

He turns to look at Steven.

"You can stay if you like. All of this can be yours."

The ride reaches its climax, and begins the descent again, steadily, shuddering and clanging uneasily.

Steven looks down. The lights dim, muted and sickly, garish paint fading and metal staining with rust, rides growing creaky and clanking. The ride car going forever up and down and up. The carnival below is ruined, deserted, and goes dark. His friends have all gone home. The garish lights a flashing memory, fading with the off-key steam organ music and whiz-zing bell-ringing chaotic clamor of the midway.

He looks up at the man.

"But I don't want it. I don't want to be here."

"This is your last chance," the man says with a wicked grin. "Just shake my hand."

"Are you giving it to me free?"

"Nothing is free."

"Then I would have to pay. I don't have any money. I'm just a little boy."

"I'll tell you what." The man's eyes narrow. "Give me the change in your pocket. I heard it jingle. I know it's there. A bit of silver and a handshake, and we have a deal."

Steven reaches into his pocket and pulls out half a dozen coins, dropping some of them on the ground, staring at them in his hand, surprised they are there.

The man points at a penny then a nickel.

"That will do."

He is standing on the ground, the man next to him so tall, the dark and silent carnival looming all around.

The man pulls out a piece of paper, holding it out.

"Just sign here, and all this is yours."

Steven looks at the paper, then up at the man.

"I still don't want it."

The man brandishes a sharply pointed feather quill.

"Just sign on the damned line. A drop of blood is all I need. See?"

He pokes his own finger with the quill, a bead of blood seeping to the surface, and with a flourish signs his own name to the paper, the writing unreadable.

"You will be free from everything. No consequences, no conscience. To do as you please. You will be free from your family, your mother endlessly calling your name."

"Steeeven," an unseen voice hisses in the silent darkness, the name hoarse, drawn out. The sound brings a new chill to his flesh, digging deeper than the icy fingers of the cool air.

"You will be free to have all this." The man waves his arm, palm up, bead of blood still on his finger, to encompass the carnival and all that lies beyond.

"But you said nothing is free," Steven says.

"It's all free," the showman says with a wide grin.

Hesitantly, Steven takes the quill and pricks his finger.

He looks up at the showman, and
the man is Steven.

Author Inspiration

Alice Cooper, the king of shock rock and pioneer of gothic-drenched heavy metal, was my first favorite rock star. As someone who always loved darker stories, his music and dark theatrics spoke to me on a level no other group or musician has.

He was the first concert I saw. Me, an utterly inescapably, fully-introverted youth, surprised with a "Let's go" from my older brother, who seldom had much to do with his younger siblings. My utterly confused "Where?" Followed by the mind- and body-numbing "Alice Cooper."

I was in a fairytale. The hugeness of the relatively small arena, by arena standards. I'd never been. The crowds and air tingling with excitement and an air of expectant wonder which everyone in the place seemed to share. It was intimidating, but I knew I was safe with my brother.

The stage was a marvelous thing. And, when Alice Cooper strutted out on that stage in costume, sporting somewhat disturbing makeup I knew would earn my mother's disapproval, and started singing and performing what I'd have best described as a magically dark musical play if I'd had the words then, I was in awe.

Art, in all its forms, is a visceral creature. Some pieces, stories, visual art, and music, stirring different senses, touch on a deeper level. Certain Alice Cooper songs did that.

When I saw a submission call for Dismember the Coop, I was thrilled to learn it was not about dismembered birds. An Alice Cooper tribute horror anthology? I'm all in! This was going to be fun to write, even if I didn't make the cut. Being a charity anthology for the Solid Rock Teen Centers made it a worthy cause.

Welcome to My Nightmare was always my favorite Cooper album. And, from the soft tinkling piano and small voice, the darkly twisted story, the character's strained confusion, to the wails of "Steeeven," the saga of Steven sprinkled through Cooper's songs and albums intrigued me.

"Carnival Ride" is based on Steven's saga and some of the interpretations of Cooper's songs. The mistreated little boy who becomes

"Caffeine"

by Ross Baxter

Dr Ella Cortez arrived early at the small research building on the outskirts of Phoenix; she knew the day was going to be long and wanted to get it started as soon as she possibly could. The drive in had been unusually quiet, with little traffic, and no waiting at the numerous roadblocks, but even more remarkable had been the complete absence of infected. Normally, she would encounter at least two or three on the thirty-minute commute from the compound she now called home, usually lurking in the overgrown front gardens or running blindly at the car. But not today, which she took to be a good omen.

She nodded to Vince, the heavily-armed night security guard who cautiously opened the heavy gate to the carpark, and drove the battered Ford inside to a halt in the yellow-hatched disabled parking slot. On a normal day she would have not used the space, even though she was the only employee working there actually registered as disabled. She did not want to be thought as being any different from her colleagues, despite having a leg amputated above the knee following a bite.

She actually felt lucky and believed having a parking space meaningless. Being bit usually resulted in the quick onset of feral psychosis, the com-plete loss of higher-mental functions, and final reversion to a carnivorous animalistic state. In her case, the quick-thinking action of Vince, firstly to decapitate the infected biter with a fire axe, and secondly to completely sever her leg above the bite, stopped the spread of the virus in her body. Her colleagues then managed to stem the blood loss, and patch her up enough to save her life. Ella felt both lucky and thankful and would gladly give up the parking space anyday to Vince, if he actually owned a car. But today, for the first time, she parked the car in the hatched area, happy to shave a few seconds from what she knew would be a marathon.

Although the drinking of coffee had been prohibited in the facility three months earlier, she still craved that early morning caffeine hit, but had no option other than ignore it. She moved quickly up the steps despite her prosthetic leg and opened the door into the empty reception area of the facility.

The heavy smell of disinfectant hit her as she entered. Glaring bright lights came on automatically as she marched down the deserted barren corridors to the secure laboratories at the rear of the building. Opening the armoured door took much longer than the other openings, this one requiring card, voice confirmation, and even a retina scan. Finally, the huge door swung open, wafting the strong stench of rotting flesh and defecation over her. Although enough to make even the strongest gag, after all the time she had spent in the complex, she no longer noticed it. Neither did she pay attention to the pitiful cries of the recently infected from the ten holding cells within, where she finally stopped.

All ten cells were occupied: five on the left, and five on the right. The naked occupants in the left-hand cells, all having been infected for many months, hissed savagely at her, skeletal arms clawing through the bars, putrid and tumorous. These creatures, no longer human, were beyond any help she could give except the mercy of a bullet. Craving only human flesh, they existed only to kill and feed.

She ignored the wretches and focussed on the occupants of the right-hand cells. Having been more recently infected, these still retained a semblance of speech and some rudimentary human reasoning, but only just, and what little they had kept slipping away with each passing hour. Those in the first four cells shrieked and roared at her, banging their bleeding fists against the cold metal bars in anger, frustration, and hunger. The occupant in the fifth cell remained sullenly seated on the stained mattress, silently staring at Ella. She stared back at the infected woman's filthy nakedness, inwardly fighting the guilt she felt.

"Cindy, I'm so sorry we have to treat you this way. You know we have to do it as part of our research, to make sure you're in exactly the same environment as the other controlled subjects."

The young woman said nothing, returning her gaze to the dirty tiled floor.

"But it's all been worth it, Cindy. You've been on the treatment for two weeks now and have stabilised, and you're not deteriorating like the others. It's a real breakthrough, and, I believe, this is actually the start of a real cure. All we have to do now is persuade the powers that be to continue our funding."

"How could you?" Cindy cried, hatred in her bloodshot blue eyes. "We were friends once, and you keep me caged here like an animal!"

"You got bitten and infected whilst working here in the labs," explained Ella. "But with all our work we've now got something that could be a future cure. It needs more work, but look what you'd be like without it, like the others in these cages. As long as we keep you medicated, you remain sane and human."

"I'm eighteen, I'm like a teenage Frankenstein. I can't live in this nightmare!" Cindy shrieked, waving away the halo of flies which circled her in the stinking cell. "Help me, for the love of God!"

"If you weren't here, the authorities would have euthanized you by now. You know that being here is the best for you, and for everyone," answered Ella calmly. "The control phase is now over. We'll clean you up, get you some clothes, and move you to another room, on your own. We'll still have to keep you locked up, until we're sure you won't relapse. I've also got a small

task for you to do, but if you co-oper-
ate, I think your nightmare is almost
over. You are the future."

Ella turned to depart, but inadver-
tently strayed too close to the cage
next to Cindy's. A thin arm whipped
out through the rusted bars, grabbing her arm in a vice-like grip. She
struggled but the grip held, pulling her
towards the cage and the gnashing
bloody teeth of the infected lunatic
within. The second arm joined the
first, latching hold of her below the
elbow and doubling the force. Bracing
her good leg against the bottom of the
bars, she pushed back against the pull,
halting the movement but still unable
to pull away or break the iron grip.

"Vince!" she screamed, knowing how unlikely she was to be heard.

Using her cell phone would be almost impossible one-handed, and the only other thing she had in her pockets were her keys. Keeping her legs firmly braced against the bars, she gripped the keys tightly with her free hand, the long serrated edge of the facility entrance key facing out. She slashed it against the filthy thin arm of her caged assailant, again and again, hoping the pain would loosen the unassailable grip. But apart from increased screeching, the slashes had no effect, and the infected creature held firm. Instead of wildly slashing, Ella switched the angle of the keys and tried to concentrate on sawing at one area, attempting to cut through the tendons and muscles.

Panicked minutes passed, the screams of the infected now deafening and the pain from the grip increasing, and Ella started to tire. Despite the keys having sliced through inches of muscle, almost down to the bone, the shrieking infected grasping her showed no sign of letting go. Then, covered in glutinous dark blood, the keys slipped out of her clutch and clattered to the tiled floor, well out of reach.

"Throw me your phone!" yelled Cindy.

Ella reached into her pocket and yanked out the phone, tossing it low towards Cindy's cage.

"The code's 124578," she cried. "Call Vince, his number is in the contacts!"

Instead of weakening, the pull of the infected seemed to be getting stronger. This was one of the things which made them so dangerous; they were largely oblivious to grievous injuries and able to keep going long after a normal human would have succumbed to pain or blood loss. Ella's legs felt weak, and she had long lost the feeling in her arm below the tight grip which pulled her progressively closer and closer to the bars and the horrific gaping yaw of broken biting teeth.

Suddenly, the door to the lab burst open, and Vince rushed in, fire axe in hand. Without a word he raised the heavy axe and swung it quickly down. It skittered down the bars, sparks flying, separating both hands of the infected at the wrists, before smashing noisily into the cracked tile floor. Ella threw herself backwards, the ghastly hands still fastened tight below her elbows. The infected continued to thrust the stumps of both arms blindly forwards, seemingly oblivious to the loss of its hands.

"Let me help you with those," panted Vince, prising off the dead hands with his strong dark fingers.

Ella nodded gratefully, trying to control her panicked breathing and moving away from the other cages and reaching arms. "Where would I be without you and your fire axe?"

"Or me on your phone," croaked Cindy, half-heartedly trying to cover her nakedness from Vince.

"Exactly," wheezed Ella. "Thank you both."

"You're the only one in this screwed-up world who seems to be making any headway on a cure," replied Vince. "I've got to protect you."

Ella shook her head, wiping the dark gluey blood from her arms. "Right now, it's Cindy who's the important one. We've got to administer all her doses, and it's vital we get them exactly right today. Then we get her cleaned up and ready to go."

"Go where?" said Vince and Cindy, simultaneously.

"The state capital," said Ella. "It's time to make them listen."

Professor James Dalby let out a deep sigh as he scanned the research paper open on his desk, forlornly looking for any sign that the vast amount of money being poured into the research was having any effect. He doubted the file would be any different to the hundreds of other reports he had already seen, but he had a responsibility to keep looking. It was a gruelling and soul-destroying duty, one seemingly with no end.

The sound of the telephone stirred him, and he picked it up with another heavy sigh.

"Doctor Ella Cortez and her assistant are here, from Arizona State University," his secretary announced cheerily.

"Just send Cortez in, I haven't got time to meet a delegation," Dalby snapped irritably. Cortez was his fifth appointment of the day, and it was not yet mid-morning. "And can you make me a coffee, please? A very strong one."

The door opened after a moment, and a dishevelled-looking woman walked hesitantly in. Middle-aged and in an ill-fitting business suit, to Dalby she looked no different than the countless other academics who had walked into the office over the past few months.

"Please take a seat," Dalby said, rising unenthusiastically to shake her hand.

"Thank you for seeing me," said Ella with sincerity. "I've been really looking forward to updating you on the fantastic progress of my research team. I just wish the circumstances were different; the announcement of possible funding cuts in research is not doing our morale any good at all."

Dalby nodded, having heard the same thing from every academic he had seen in recent months. "I'm afraid, Doctor Cortez, that regarding funding cuts, the word is 'definite', not 'possible'."

"But it's absolutely unbelievable that they can even consider reducing research funding!" blurted Ella.

Dalby sternly looked at her over the rim of his spectacles.

"How both our government and the World Health Organisation can justify wanting to put the brakes on research simply defies all logic," she continued to rant bitterly. "We're still a long way from finding a scientific solution to the global epidemic!"

"That's exactly the point of why they're doing it!" Dalby shot back, trying in vain to control his irritation. "I haven't got time to debate ethics with you, but the simple fact is that the epidemic is actually only being beaten with guns and brute force! Just look at where we are; Australia, New Zealand, Japan, and Scandinavia are all clean now, as are most of the southern U.S. states. But they've eradicated the virus not with science, but with military curfews, bombs, and bullets. Science has contributed nothing so far, despite the huge amount of cash poured into research. There is simply not enough money left in the economies to keep ploughing into hopeless projects."

"Surely you can't mean that, Professor Dalby? You can't be saying that it is better to invest in killing rather than curing? We're scientists, with a social conscience," she retorted dumbly, visibly taken aback by the professor's stance. "Science is a community, we work together as a world-wide co-op. Clearly, we must all keep working together until a cure is found!"

Dalby regarded her coldly, knowing he would have to explain again for the fifth time that morning. "Science was a co-op, but the epidemic has brought the world to its knees, and that nicety has effectively been dismembered.

We're in the worst global recession since the dark ages, the population of the planet has more than halved, and many survivors are now starting to regard scientists like pariahs. They believe the scientific community have failed to come up with answers, and now the population increasingly looks to the military as their saviours. Only brute force is having any effect on stopping the epidemic, and so that is where the money is increasingly being channelled.

"It's simple economics. The government doesn't want any more trouble than it's already got. It's no longer about staying elected, it's about preventing total collapse, like what has happened in England. Rebellion and anarchy is not what anyone wants."

"But my team has made a real breakthrough!" Ella cut in.

Dalby raised his eyebrows sceptically. Every research team told him the same thing, but when it came down to it, their breakthroughs always proved minor or insignificant.

"My team at the Arizona State University branch here in Phoenix are using concentrated caffeine extracted from coffee beans to control the behaviour of the infected. It really is working!" she enthused.

"Caffeine!" Dalby snorted in derision and shook his head. He opened the file on Cortez's research and scanning down the summary page. "Your university was given a grant of funds just over six months ago. Half a million dollars committed, and you're telling me you're using that money to see if the infected like to drink coffee?"

"No, of course not!" Ella yelped. "We inject them with strictly measured and controlled amounts of caffeine. We've found that a certain dosage completely changes their behaviour. They become docile, pliant, and controllable; no longer intent on killing and feeding. More importantly, it stops further deterioration of the higher neural powers. It's all in the file you're holding. Caffeine is the solution to the epidemic!"

"Stop right there," warned Dalby sternly. "This is exactly why people are losing faith in science! You're saying that we just have to capture the infected, inject them with measured doses of caffeine, and that'll keep them docile until their next fix. What sort of a ridiculous answer is that?"

"It's a breakthrough!" asserted Ella angrily.

Dalby tiredly closed the file and put it to one side. "Can't you see what's happening? I grew up with the certain and unassailable belief that the pen was mightier than the sword. People and society had a real conviction that science provided the only workable solutions to mankind's problems, not religion, not force, and not ignorance.

"But the failure of science to stop or control this nightmare epidemic is changing that conviction: people are now turning their back on academics and science. More and more are coming to the conclusion that the bullet is mightier than the test tube. Scientists are starting to be ridiculed; we'll soon be ranked lower than tax inspectors, realtors, and even anthology editors in the league table of the most derided professions. The new Dark Ages are coming, and you sit there and try to persuade me that coffee therapy is the best that science can come up with!

Billions of dollars of research to say that Starbucks is actually the answer!"

"You've obviously not read my paper."

"Don't insult my intelligence," Dalby ranted. "This meeting is over. I've turned down four other teams for further funding this morning, and none of their research was as harebrained as yours. You won't be getting any more funding from the State of Arizona, the US Federal Government, or from the World Health Organisation. Good day!"

"Wait!" Ella cried defiantly. "All the proof you need is just outside. I didn't bring an associate with me, I brought an infected. Her name is Cindy, and she was a research student who got bitten in the lab almost three weeks ago. She is the one who proved our theories. We've experimented on dozens and dozens of infected subjects, but finally we got it right with Cindy.

"The key is getting the dosage set exactly for the subject's body mass and metabolism. Too little and it has no effect, too much and it makes them worse. But I've dosed her with an exact amount of caffeine, and she is now sitting quietly right outside this door. You wouldn't know she was infected; I've walked her past security and through the whole building like any normal person. She looks normal, she can hold a rational conversation, and she has absolutely no desire to tear anybody's head off. I'll bring her in so you can see for yourself what effect an exact controlled dose of caffeine has on the infected."

"What!" Dalby cried. He stared at Ella in shocked disbelief, his hand reaching for the loaded revolver in his desk drawer.

"Don't worry," Ella continued. "I know the exact dose of caffeine she needs. This is what we've been working on. I've given her the right amount of caffeine that will keep her pliant for another two hours at least."

"Are you out of your mind?" stuttered Dalby. "What happens to the exact dosage if my secretary offers her a coffee?"

Ella looked at him in sudden consternation. She made to reply, but Dalby's question was answered by the sound of smashing china, maniacal roars, and hysterical screaming from the other side of the office door.

Author Inspiration

Alice Cooper is not only a survivor of the massive and often negative changes in the music industry since his career started back in 1964, but he has thrived and been a beacon in the darkness. I wanted the story to reflect that: apocalypses can happen, but human nature is all about pushing through.

"The Recital of Bones"
by Bernardo Villela

Kelly stood at the kitchen counter, hands in his coat pockets; instead of his house keys, he dug out a metacarpal. It slipped out of his hand and skittered across the countertop. He lunged out to retrieve it but missed. It crashed into a stack of mail he'd not checked yet. The first envelope looked like it might contain a check. Kelly ripped it open with one finger.

"Uncle Merle! Check!" Kelly called out. Merle's social security payment had come in.

Kelly was glad. His own social security wouldn't be in for more than a decade, but he felt he had more than earned his keep for all the time spent caring for his family.

"Check," Merle echoed.

Kelly chuckled. "It's like living with a parrot."

"Parrot," Merle repeated.

Kelly belly-laughed, then picked up the metacarpal and tucked it into his pocket. It wouldn't do to leave it here. Kelly felt something else in his pocket and fished out the keys to his old Pontiac.

Why do I still carry these around?

He put them back in his pocket, not wanting to face memories of him and William and their too-short time together. To forget his eternal heartbreak, Kelly went to visit Merle, who was feeling talkative.

A single bright shaft shone into the living room; one of the tapestries that blacked out the windows was sagging.

"That can't be good," Kelly said, adjusting the curtain so the outside world remained shut out as he wanted it.

Having returned a pall of darkness to the room, Kelly faced Merle.

Long had Merle sat skinless on that musty loveseat, unmoving even as he repeated Kelly's words, yet the dark enlivened him as if he'd become nocturnal. Merle had liked this room during his life, so much that he had died there, but just now, Kelly avoided thinking of that.

"Better," Kelly said to himself seeing Merle seated comfortably. Then, on the way out, he said over his shoulder, "See you at dinner, Merle."

Kelly glanced at his wristwatch, an old habit of his. It was dead, had been dead for a while, like so much else in his life. He clambered into the corridor that split the house and saw the grandfather clock read 4:15 p.m.

At the end of the hall, he approached a door flaking lead paint.

Kelly opened that door and left it gaping—another old habit, this one developed in childhood, because it was always safer in case he had to escape. Memories played in the dark as he gazed down the blackened staircase, but only for a moment, until Kelly put them away like bones he didn't want to leave out. Then he proceeded down into the chilled, earthen basement.

The bare lightbulb that hung from a chain was dark, but Kelly knew how to weave his way through the graves of those he had shunned. He thought of them as The Humps, since they protruded from the ground. The buried no longer spoke. But between their burial and the moment they had died, they unleashed vile torrents of hatred into Kelly's mind. It was those spirits Kelly wanted silenced as soon as possible.

The far righthand corner was the only part of the basement where some linoleum tiling remained intact. On that sat the chest freezer.

Opening the freezer's lid, Kelly saw within it a clash of order and chaos: cuts of meat—once organized—were strewn about. He had enough to get through a nuclear winter and another COVID uptick, or any other pandemic he might have to endure, and there was still room for his newest body: Anne. She gazed dead-eyed and frozen at Kelly as he gazed into the case.

"Hello, Kelly," she said through frozen, still lips.

"Hi, Anne," he replied. "I'll warm ya soon enough."

"When?"

Kelly hesitated, thinking about those who shared the space with him upstairs and how it was past time someone had to move out.

"Soon. I'm working on it."

Kelly snapped an icicle off a tomahawk steak and took the meat from the icebox.

"Promise?"

"Promise."

The lid slammed shut against the emanating cold.

On his way out, Kelly ran between The Humps, not deigning to look down at those who no longer deserved to remain above ground, and he charged up the stairs.

In the kitchen, he was laying the tomahawk out to thaw on the counter, when the wall phone jangled hatefully, breaking Kelly's peaceful silence. The caller ID's robotic voice informed him it was Dr. Rotund. Kelly waited for the ringing to stop, his thoughts clattering into one another, shattering from the impact. Rage threatened to overtake him, so to keep control, he began his ritual Recital of Bones.

Aunt Catherine's nearly gone. Leg-bones pulverized, sprinkled on the lawn. Arm-bones sledgehammered, at

....

The ringing ended.

When family members stayed with Kelly after departing life, he'd first burn off their fingerprints. When there was no more skin left to salvage, he pulled out their teeth. Storm drains were great disposal sites for them. Then they could live with him anew, without causing Kelly undue issues. This also calmed their postmortem rages.

When he could function again, Kelly opened the fridge and removed all the vegetables. After putting them in a stockpot to stew, he knew he'd have to play the voicemail. There was always the faint possibility Dr. Rotund's concern might lead to a word to the authorities that Kelly had eluded so far.

"Kelly," Dr. Rotund said in a full, kind voice. Kelly was jarred. He expected an automated message about being overdue for his refill.

"I missed you last week," Dr. Rotund continued. "Thought I'd check in. I know you don't want to hear from robots. You also don't want me playing Dr. Pillpusher. But I *do* want to speak to you. Per my records, you're current on all meds but Thorazine. If you want it phased out, we need to talk." Dr. Rotund feared Kelly was no longer on speaking terms with reality. Kelly knew the doctor harbored that fear but thought he'd find the truth more disturbing. "Going cold turkey all of a sudden isn't—anyway, call me. You're still on the schedule. And I waived the no-show fee. Bye."

Kelly debated going to next week's appointment. It froze him.

"*Like me?*" Anne called from the basement.

Kelly ignored her taunts. It wasn't a decision he needed to make now. At that moment, he wished he could hide in his room. During previous periods without Thorazine, if the clamoring of his dead relatives became too in-cessant, his bedroom had served as a sanctuary from their torture.

As much as Kelly would like a sanctuary now, he had to move on. Besides, getting back into his routine would be a better salve for his mind.

Dinner was one of his favorite daily activities. The table was set for five despite only Kelly actually eating. Onto the four spare plates he plopped a ladleful of stewed vegetables, though on his own plate, Kelly would take on the tomahawk alone. Then he proceeded to eat from the other dishes. There was no one else to eat the vegetables. The remainder of his dinner party was dead. Regardless, they spoke to him. They'd been better conversationalists in the past, but it was still better than eating alone.

Where Kelly and Dr. Rotund disagreed was on the nature of the voices. The doctor thought they were manifestations of schizophrenia that needed to be eradicated.

"*How was your day, Kelly?*" the voice drifting from his extreme left asked.

"It was good, Ma," Kelly answered.

Kelly didn't think the voices were figments of his imagination, he believed his loved ones were still speaking to him and Thorazine muffled their voices. Looking at his mother wearing her hospital gown unsettled him. She hadn't done that since she was getting used to being among the family again, for the most part she'd been her stylish self.

"Still a lot to do to move Aunt Catherine out," Kelly said, trying to keep his cool.

Had Dr. Rotund known what Kelly's house was like, he'd understand Kelly's conviction. But Kelly knew Dr. Rotund could never know, because then confidentiality would no longer bind him.

"<u>Anne still bothering you?</u>" asked a voice directly in front of him.

"Yeah, Dad."

Kelly's father wore his undershirt, his face bearing shaving creme and fresh nicks. Kelly fell silent chewing on some gristle, trying to understand why everyone was off.

"You gotta clean up better," a sweet, seraphic voice teased him, speaking right into his ear. He couldn't breathe, couldn't recite bones, he just had to look right. Kelly smirked, seeing Freddie's smiling face just as he always remembered it. Kelly grimaced; Freddie's presence was always bittersweet.

"I think I'll eat Freddie's veggies first tonight," Kelly announced to the room's spirits. The attempt at levity didn't cheer Kelly up. Instead, it allowed Freddie's final moments to invade Kelly's mind. That memory was one he blocked out several times a day.

"Kelly!" gurgled someone directly to his left. The angry, scratchy, phlegm-clogged voice was what he least wanted to hear. He saw Aunt Catherine's limp neck laid on her shoulder, blood pouring from her mouth, nose, and ears.

Kelly fell back, choking on his tomahawk, unrendered fat caught in his throat. He fell out of his chair. A few hacks. He bit down on the expelled beef, finally able to chew it. With that chunk of meat swallowed, he knew he was done with his meal.

Kelly wouldn't lie to his mother, even after she died. He <u>did</u> have a lot to do that night after dinner, but after the meal's unpleasant turn, he knew he'd need to relax before leaving home.

"Being a bundle of nerves never made things easier" was a truism of his mother's he'd recited his whole life, even after he moved her remains out of the house—an event that proved more imminent than he'd thought.

Kelly poured himself a snifter of cognac and put on a Louis Armstrong record. He wished to savor his drink, but when he heard Satchmo singing "C'est si bones," he knew he'd find no peace at home.

"Might as well get busy," he said, standing up while downing the cognac.

Getting Aunt Catherine out will calm Anne and me both.

He traipsed across the living room into the foyer. Kelly opened the coat closet door. Reaching in for walking shoes, he pulled out moccasins instead, deciding he'd rather wear them. His father liked wearing them around the house and had bought many pairs from Chippewa artisans through the years. Kelly thought of those endearing moments that ran counter to his father's usual demeanor whenever he almost gave up on the ghost, ignoring the fact that those moccasins got cared for better than he and his mother at times. Except, of course, when Dad had finally had it.

As he put one on, a metatarsal slid out. Kelly picked it up and put it into his coat pocket.

"Dad, you didn't tell me you left a toe in here," he said back toward the table.

His father didn't respond.

Kelly wasn't surprised his dad had left a souvenir behind in the moccasin. His family didn't mind being around for the most part, but they had no inter-est in making his life easier.

Dusk inched toward night as Kelly exited his house. He was immediately faced with his old Pontiac. Its lifeless bulk sat parked in front of their house. Another persistent reminder of William and of the final time he felt whole.

That's why Kelly still clung onto them, because they were a part of him, a part of William, the only one in the house who still made him feel loved.

Kelly's part of town never thrived, never had a renaissance, and its best days were long gone. Many lots on the street were now vacant, abandoned, or condemned. That desolation comforted Kelly, which was why he was *discomforted* seeing so many people out and about on the street.

<u>Where'd they come from?</u>

As he turned left and started walking, he realized they were souls, not people.

Three doors down stood a crumbling brick edifice which had housed many failed businesses but was still referred to as <u>The Tribune Building</u>. Most recently it had been squatted in by the homeless. Lying on its front doorstep was Norman, who Kelly was certain had died of exposure last winter.

Kelly shuffled past Norman, disregarding whatever the man shouted into the cold-crackled night air. Kelly's hands sought warmth in his coat pockets but found only the chill-trapping old bones. Suddenly, a soft, childlike voice called from the darkness. It was Freddie's voice from when they were both young. But when Kelly envisioned his brother's face, it was not as he wished to recall it—as it had been forty-two years ago: peach-pink, blue-eyed, and bright—but as he loathed to remember: pallid, sweaty, and riddled with smallpox.

"Freddie, what're you doing here?"

"<u>You have my finger.</u>"

Kelly knew his brother was right. He sprinted to avoid looking at the ugliness of Freddie's death. He had one family member to see off tonight.

Panic is an absurd state of being, because you can never tell what will snap you out of it. The bitterness of Kelly's past had set him on edge, but something as simple as a DON'T WALK sign offered him a moment's reprieve. He stopped himself from stepping into the crosswalk. Then he heard something that chilled him anew.

"BOOOOOOY!"

If he'd moved on, he wouldn't have heard his father's death-bellow coming from the past. If he'd moved on—but he hadn't. Unable to stop himself, he looked right and saw his father staggering about. Kelly cringed. Then he saw his mother and his younger self.

"Dad, you're drunk, leggo!" he heard his younger self shriek hysterically.

"Bruce! Listen to him, put it down!" he heard his mother say.

The resounding boom that followed Kelly knew too well.

His younger self reached for the shotgun in his father's hands.

"Don't touch it!" Kelly's mother shouted, not to his younger self who grabbed the gun, but to his current self, who was watching the past transpire. His younger self knew his father would fight him for the shotgun, what he hadn't anticipated was his father taking it from him and pointing the muzzle at his own face.

Kelly's mother stared right at him, ignoring the scene that had played out many times before.

He ran from the vision, across the street. Looking over his shoulder, Kelly saw his father's head was whole again, shotgun back in his hands—then the fight started over.

Kelly's father turned the shotgun toward his own head. Kelly'd had both hands around the gun's stock, not the barrels. Kelly's father twisted Young Kelly's wrist.

A resonant boom followed. His father's head bloomed out, into a bloody muffin-top of blood, bone splinters, and brain matter.

Kelly whipped his head around. He wished he'd not worn the moccasins, not brought his dad along with him.

Leaving the vision behind, he knew he needed to not only get Aunt Catherine's presence in his life tonight but get back to work tomorrow. In the meantime, Kelly wended his way through the more populous but no less dodgy parts of town. Local recycling centers and landfills were all familiar to Kelly now. Walking to a Styrofoam processing facility, he engaged in The Recital of Bones.

Aunt Catherine's nearly gone. Leg-bones pulverized, sprinkled on the lawn. Arm-bones sledgehammered at dawn, ribcage shattered, mingled with a fawn.

"You're an ass, Kelly, and you always have been!" Aunt Catherine said to him through her bones.

"I'm doing the best I can, Aunt Catherine," he grumbled at her, trying his damnedest to keep his cool.

"Has it been worth it, Kelly?"

Many things in Kelly's surroundings were in disrepair. The chain-link fence around the recycling facility was dented, perforated, and ill-guarded. When

232

so many around him seemed to give up on life, it facilitated Kelly living in the past.

He opened the baggie and scattered her minuscule remnants: hand, foot, and inner-ear bones among the white debris.

"How long do you think it can last?" she asked him.

Kelly turned and walked off without answering the question, urgency in his gait. He was convinced he was right to stop the Thorazine. His family members had likely been clamoring for a while, but he had been deaf to their pleas.

Kelly felt himself getting more fragile the whole way home. His feet hitting the pavement shocked his skeleton, squeezed his heart, and thumped his head. The way back was just as long, but a slower go. Pain, physical and psychic, expanded from his core like a nuclear bomb detonating. And it lingered.

Shadows slinked around him as if sentient, keeping peace at bay. Kelly wanted to believe that reaching his street would end the fright-show, but he knew it would not be so. Having left home, the players in his own private Grand Guignol were more inclined to improvise.

The memory of Aunt Catherine continued to speak to him: "How long do you think it can last?"

Kelly recited again to get his aunt's phantasm out of his head. Before he knew it, he was back near home and the abandoned <u>Tribune</u> building. He saw Freddie's pock-marked face glowing before a trashcan fire. Kelly's breathing shallowed as he looked at his brother and squeezed the finger-bone that rested in his pocket.

<u>Freddie gets to stay, Freddie needs to play, no bones yet to put away.</u>

The incantation soothed his nerves—that was until he heard a booming, "<u>BOOOOOOY!</u>"

Kelly saw his father. He wasn't reenacting his death this time but coming at him. Father coming at him, not on some ectoplasmic stage, was new.

Ripples of fear crashed through him, and this new development made him run for his life.

"HEY! BOOOOOOY, DON'T RUN AWAY FROM ME!"

Kelly tried to keep reciting, but—

Where're the house keys?

He could hear his father's footsteps pounding the pavement.

Digging in his pockets: finger-bone, toe-bone, unmatched glove, breath mints. No keys. He ran on. He was nearly home when he pulled the keys to the Pontiac out of his pocket again. It wasn't what he wanted. Despair fell on him for a moment, but Kelly realized he didn't have time for that. The door to his house was closed and the ghostly footsteps were growing louder. He had no choice. Giving in, he jumped into his car, locking the door behind him.

The grave sound of fist-falls on his window was drowned out when Kelly locked the car doors. It was replaced by something he wanted to face even less than that. So many memories of William and their time together lingered in this car. So many instances of their brief period of freedom, the end of which reset his life.

Kelly and William had been friends since they were kids. In grade school it was often just the two of them, there were no playgrounds within walking distance. So they played games kids normally played in mixed company like House and Doctor.

Growing older they clung to each other, navigating adolescent pitfalls. Groping blindly, they did what was expected of them, unsure why they couldn't find any happiness. Neither of them realized their true feelings for one another until a long time after.

That changed when they went to see <u>The Silence of the Lambs</u>. Looking back, it was easy to see how they set things up, how an increased intimacy was a long time coming. Their eyes were locked on the screen, transfixed and terrified. Kelly reached for their shared popcorn bucket between William's legs. He missed. Kelly didn't remove his hand; William reciprocated.

One obstacle in accepting their sexuality was the sentiment Kelly and William shared: "Maybe we don't like guys, just each other." Kelly and William didn't insist on exclusivity. Free to explore their sexuality, they both went wild. One day, William found the wrong partner. One whose postcoital guilt turned him violent.

William had managed to drag himself to a payphone and call Kelly for help. Somehow, Kelly had sped to William's side fast enough to weep into William's warm blood as it ran from stab wounds in his chest. With his dying breaths, William told Kelly it was

Troy who'd done it. Kelly buried Troy in the first of The Humps.

Teary-eyed Kelly stormed out of his car, out of the past. He lifted his coat, reached into his jeans-pocket. Found the key, unlocked the door, prepared to face the new nightmare awaiting in the living room.

Kelly's bleached mother stood before him, pointing an accusatory bony digit.

"There you are my boy. Atone!"

He didn't need his mother's sermonizing; he needed a drink. He barged past her, swatting her supernaturally suspended arm away.

"I MEAN IT!" she roared, grabbing his wrist. "Or we'll put you in The

Humps." Her hand was cold and hard and possessed a vivacious strength.

He looked into her empty eye sockets as if her dulcet, honey-brown eyes still resided there. In those black voids Kelly saw her being wheeled away on a gurney into an operating room.

"Yes, I died on the table," she said in a rattling whisper.

Kelly pulled his arm out of his mother's hand. He expected all her bones to crumble, but freeing himself didn't break whatever mysterious power kept her up and about.

"Did Dr. Rotund put you up to this?"

"He doesn't have to ever discover we're out if you put us away."

Kelly turned his back to her.

241

He decided to visit Anne. She'd been a pain earlier, but at least she'd been one when she was alive as well. Kelly would rather spend time with her and those he'd put in The Humps for splintering his family.

"Kelly!"

The voice had such a timbre, such vibrato, it rattled his bones. He'd never heard anything, nor anyone, so terrifying. Hell, it could be the Devil himself for all he knew.

Kelly turned. It was Merle, who was also on his feet.

It'd been so long since Merle had been anything but a jovial echo, Kelly couldn't recognize his uncle's voice beneath its anger and shock, tones he'd not heard Merle utter since he was bitter, coked-out, and on his way to an overdose after being laid-off.

The skeleton of a man shambled his way. He reached out and brushed against Kelly's arm, but Kelly didn't let himself get grabbed by the phalanges.

Kelly fled but stopped before the basement door. There he knew he'd witness visions of Anne's death; he'd see again how he punished those he'd put in The Humps. He couldn't bear it, not again, not after the torments he'd faced already. He needed the safety of his bed. He needed it more than any-thing ever before.

Kelly closed the bedroom door. There was an instant of quiet, then came clacking and thudding behind him. Old, unspoken agreements were broken, for bony fists pounded in protest.

How many? Four?

"Going to sleep!" he informed them.

Kelly slid into his bed. On the pillow next to him lay the sweetest skull in the house, his William. Unlike those at the threshold, whose patience was exhausted, never a cross word passed between the two of them. Even as Kelly's family tired, William was his steadfast companion beneath the sheets. The sight of him calmed Kelly.

Only loving eyes could see that small frame swaddled in satin pajamas and feel affection instead of being repulsed by the absurdity of the sight.

Kelly turned off the lamp on his nightstand. Blue moonlight flowed through the window. As always, he laid down and held William's hand without hesitation.

"<u>Kelly</u>!" It was his mother.

"<u>Kelly</u>!" Merle now.

"<u>KELLY</u>!" His father.

Kelly's heart shuddered, expecting a gunshot, and he could swear he heard a fourth fist in the chorus of knocks.

"<u>KELLLLY</u>!" Anne called out. He didn't know if she spoke from the freezer or if she stood with the skeletons outside his bedroom door. Kelly turned and looked at William. But those corn-flower-blue eyes Kelly could gaze into for an eternity were gone. There was nothing but a vacant skull.

"Kelly ..." William garbled to him at last.

"Yes?"

"Kelly ... Kelly ..."

"What?"

"You know it needs to stop, Kelly. We all need to go."

Kelly pushed William's rattling frame away.

"No, it's not true. Not you."

"I can't promise I'll be eternally brave and joyful."

"Kelly ... Kelly ... Kelly ..." chanted from the door. It had been so long since his name had bothered him.

"Do you only want to see me stabbed and bleeding, like you could only see Catherine broken-necked?"

"Kelly ..." they said at the door. William joined them.

"You want to say goodbye. Do so."

"I already said it to Aunt Cat—and how dare you? You told me to kill Troy."

"He wouldn't have gotten arrested."

"And—"

"Kelly, Kelly ..." the chant at the door continued.

"No, that's all I said."

"Kelly, Kelly, Kelly ..."

Kelly tried a new recital: <u>Catherine's gone, in the lawn, spread at dawn, mingled with a fawn, I need only William, my love; he and I are turtle doves.</u>

"<u>KELLY!</u>" the bone chorus shouted.

"What is it? Whatcha want?"

"<u>Decide</u>," William said to him.

"Decide what?"

"<u>How you want to let us go.</u>"

Kelly started weeping, understanding washing over him.

"I love you all, always have."

"<u>We know</u>," said the William that lived in Kelly's broken smile after reassuring him.

Kelly recited aloud: "<u>I need only</u> <u>William, my love; he and I are turtle</u> <u>doves.</u>"

Kelly snapped off William's right hand and formed all William's finger-bones into a makeshift dagger. Holding his beloved close, he jammed those jagged fingers into his neck, releasing a spout of arterial blood. He would hear his loved ones cries no longer but would be with them always.

Author Inspiration

When I first heard of this anthology, my initial thought was that I'd submit more than one story. One would be inspired by a more well-known song, the other would be found deeper in Alice Cooper's catalogue.

As I listened to his whole discography—the deep dive I did was deeply rewarding—my brainstorms centered on a number of his songs. He's a storyteller to the core, and many of his songs are brilliant stories already. My would-be second story was drafted but never submitted because one kept coming back to me. "Skeletons in the Closet" jumped out at me (almost literally) from its opening notes. It teased at a much bigger story than is told in that entrancing seriocomic track.

What came from my imaginings was a tale of angsts past that persist and haunt, trauma, and the stages of life. Within that framework, I included my-self and my aesthetics with those that Cooper offers, not only in this piece but his collected works. I hope you enjoyed it, and may all the fingers in your coat pocket be your own.

"The Geek"
by Madison McSweeney

These days, things to come are clearer to me than my own past. But I still remember the night I stood at the threshold of the circus, my twelve-year-old hand grasping the temporary picket fence caging the dismal wonders inside. I remember the white-and-red glow of the sideshow tent, shining brighter and sicklier than the moon. I remember the posters, garish primary colours already faded, adding an extra air of disrepute to ads for fat men and bearded women and two-headed monstrosities.

And I remember the Geek.

I was clutching my scant handful of coins—just shy of the cost of admission—when the man stumbled out from a mass of jagged shadows. His body was oddly proportioned, like old wood warped with age. His spiderlike hands struggled to restrain a frantic chicken, his eyes were yellow and wild. I was repulsed—until the moment the Geek grabbed the bird by the neck, parting his fingers just enough to fit his greedy mouth, and sank his teeth into its throat. I'm ashamed to admit, I couldn't look away.

He made short work of the chick-
en, staining his face and shirt with
blood and feathers as he devoured it
raw. My eyes followed what remained
of the carcass as it dropped to the
ground, marvelling at the profound
mutilations that had been done to it in
such a short period of time. And when
I looked up, the Geek was looking at
me. I started backwards, fearing I
would be the freak's next meal. But
when he caught my eye, I saw a cunning, conspiratorial glint in his.

The Geek raised his hand and flexed
his index finger, beckoning me closer.
As he did so, his forearm twisted like
a snake, rotating on its elbow in a way
I've never seen a human arm move

before or since. Of course, I had to comply.

I say I had to. But honestly, I hesitated. My summoner was not the most overpowering specimen of man; nonetheless, he terrified me. I had a mental image of him bearing down on me, dislocating his jaw wide enough to fit my whole head, like I'd once seen a crocodile do, and devouring me whole.

There was impatience in his manner as he once again gestured for me to follow. Like a dog on a leash, I did.

That night, the blood-spattered Geek gave me a private tour of the sideshow. The performances were done for the day, but the Geek did me one better, shepherding me through the artificial labyrinth of haphazardly parked cages and trailers. The performers, rehearsing for the next day's show, paid us no mind as they went through the motions of their acts, spitting fire, snapping up hundred-pound weights, swallowing swords. No gawking visitor disturbed us as the Geek showed me unnatural taxidermy and deformed things in jars, telling me the story of how the Ringmaster himself had sawed off the heads of aborted calves and half-born birds to be sewn onto the shoulders of other beasts—and, more horrifically, how the Queen of the Trapeze had sobbed after giving birth to a winged monstrosity, whom she immediately surrendered to the freak show and subsequently denied parentage of.

The odyssey was so fascinating, I almost forgot I'd been let in without paying. Embarrassed, I tried to thrust my meagre collection of coins into his hand, hoping I'd be able to slip away before he could count them. But the Geek caught my wrist, examined the coins, and placed them back into my palm. I stuttered a thank you and ran away.

Even though the coins never left my sight, I still instinctively counted them when I arrived home. Not only were they all there—I now had exactly enough to buy a real ticket. I want you to note how unusual this was. I'd counted my money dozens of times that afternoon before, and I'd most definitely been short. I thought I was losing my mind.

Of course, I came back the next day, and every day after.

When the circus returned the next summer, everything was different.

The gaudy colours of the freak show were gone. In their place, a palette of serene blues and greens. Where there had been shocking posters, there was now a tasteful single sign featuring an art deco image of a beautiful woman, her long tresses and delicate blue dress suggesting a mermaid—and above her, in flowery calligraphy, the words, "ASEPHONE, MYSTICAL HEAL-ER."

The only constant between this year and last was the keen yet undefined sense of trepidation I felt as I approached the sideshow tent. No Geek ushered me in this time—instead, I was received by a half dozen serene-ly smiling greeters attired in flowing summer dresses, their long hair loose, who touched my arm in a sisterly manner as they directed me inside. The interior of the tent was filled with the soft strains of an unseen harpist. Plastic chairs were arranged in rows like church pews, and a small stage had been erected at the front. I took a seat near the aisle, perhaps suspecting the need for a quick exit.

I had seen faith healing before—my mother took me along to tent revivals from time to time—but this was nothing like that at all.

The healer was a girl of perhaps twenty. She walked barefoot, and her waist-length brown hair was uncombed. She came in from under the tent flap, gently lifting it above her head as she stepped onto the stage. She hadn't spoken a word to the crowd when an orderly line began to form before her, a dozen mismatched people limping and coughing and shuffling uncomfortably from foot to foot to cane, looking at her with hope and suspicion and, perhaps above all, desperation. Among those who did not submit themselves to be healed, there was inane chatter: brash assertions of faith and skepticism; recollections of brushes with the famous evangelists of the era; earnest debates over how best to pronounce the name *Asephone.* Finally, the Ringmaster, his wild beard trimmed since last year, his top hat and tails replaced with a subdued sport coat, called for silence as the show was about to begin.

There was nothing flashy about the presentation. As each sufferer approached, Asephone would take their hands in hers. She didn't put them through the indignity of announcing their infirmities to the crowd; she let them whisper into her ear, after which she would smile kindly and place a hand on their face or forehead. A very brief trance would follow, almost imperceptible to anyone not in the first few rows.

One would be tempted to say nothing at all happened on that stage—but as each person walked away, they seemed somehow changed. One woman I watched, who had hobbled painfully to the front and waited to be healed with an expression of pure pain on her face, left her walker behind and skipped as she exited the tent.

I found the Geek behind the main tent, hosing off a lethargic-looking elephant. He seemed somehow sicker than when I'd seen him last; his skin sallower, his spine bent at an odder angle. His remaining front teeth were stained a reddish brown. His yellow eyes, however, were still bright and intelligent, and I was delighted to see he still recognized me.

Taking a seat on a cement block just out of range of the water's spray, I recounted what I'd seen. The Geek seemed irate, if engaged, and occasionally turned the hose on me when my tone turned too credulous.

"Sh-she sc-sc-scared me, a little," I added, for his benefit, still shivering from the icy blasts. His mood improved at this denunciation. Nonetheless, he pretended to be more engaged by his animal ward than my burdensome presence and didn't quiet the hose before beginning his portion of the tale.

Asephone's powers seemed to be genuine, he admitted, his hand clamping tighter around the nozzle. She had even worked her dubious magic on the freaks.

"Did she heal them?" I asked.

The Geek whirled around, scowling viciously, his back tensed as if he were about to lunge. For a moment I feared he was going to, had an image of him literally biting my head off like one of his chickens. But he calmed himself, his shoulders slumping. "In a way," he replied, his tone like a wire about to snap. "In her way."

As watery shit streamed down the leg of the elephant, the Geek told me how the Winged Man's unwanted appendages had crumbled at her touch; how he'd packed his suitcase and left soon after, pausing only to send a baleful glance towards the aging Queen of the Trapeze. The same had occurred with the Bearded Woman's facial hair, and the Fat Man, who'd requested a private meeting out of modesty, had walked out of her tent as svelte as a ballerina.

Even the performers with no obvious physical defects—the strongmen and fire-breathers and sword-swallowers— had sought her counsel. They were tight-lipped about these meetings but invariably submitted their resignations within the week, citing newly devel- oped desires for a "normal" life.

One by one, the freaks submitted themselves to be healed. And one by one, they'd taken off to parts un- known. "Lightweights," the Geek said, kicking the elephant's tree trunk leg. I laughed as the elephant indulged him. Flashing me a glimpse of those hor- rible teeth, he pivoted to hit me with the stream of cold water until I fled, equal parts terrified and thrilled.

Soon enough, stories of the healer's miraculous abilities began to spread beyond the narrow audience of circus attendees. By summer's end, it seemed that half the town had gone to see her, although few would admit it, and folks from the surrounding areas as well. I heard from my aunt that a journalist from the city was even considering making a trip. My mother, at first, resisted the siren song, unable to shake the suspicion that Asephone's powers were somehow blasphemous.

But as belief in the healer became more mainstream—an accepted fact in our community instead of a stigmatized superstition—even she came around.

"Rosemary?" she said to me one day, as I tramped into the house exhausted from a day of scouring the fields for fresh raspberries. I looked up expectantly. "Your aunt Hyacinthe was telling me about a friend of hers from the next town over. She has a little girl about your age who also has a bit of a stutter. Her mother took her to that girl at the circus..."

I stopped listening. I knew where this was going, could feel the knot of indescribable terror tighten in my stomach. I had not softened on the healer as my mother had; in fact, my fears of her seemed to grow with word of every miracle. Too good to be true, it was—it felt like a trap.

I didn't say anything to that affect, though—how could I? After all, my mother had faith and airtight anecdotal evidence, and all I had was a vague unease and the embittered word of a freak.

I said my prayers with a near hysterical fervour that night and thought repeatedly of the Geek.

And it was the Geek who I saw first when I entered the healing tent, my mother's hand clamped around mine.

I would have done a double take, convinced my eyes had deceived me, had the Geek been mistakable for anyone else. Nothing about his appearance here made any sense. Why would he submit himself to Asephone, the woman who had not only destroyed his livelihood but waged war on his kind: the pained and the strange and those beings who respectable people cross the street to avoid? And all that aside—what could he possibly want or need from her? I had never sensed any self-loathing in the Geek, but rather a strange pride. He accepted no pity and would never debase himself to be "healed."

Perhaps, I thought, he was trying to prove the healer a fraud—after all, it seemed unlikely even a miracle worker could cure whatever afflicted him. But that was a naive thought—we'd all seen her powers. I remained unconvinced that they were truly benevolent in nature, but they were far from smoke and mirrors.

The Geek was ahead of us in line, and I couldn't help but perversely wonder what would happen when Asephone laid her hands on him. Would his posture self-correct, his tics and twitches cease, his appetite bend towards fare other than raw meat?

Would he even know who he was by the end of it? And then—when all that was said and done—what would happen to <u>me</u>?

I'd had a dream the night before, which I'd tried frantically to explain to my mother. Asephone placing her finger to my lips, shushing me, speaking to me in the most soothing of tones to tell me she'd removed my stutter. I cried with happiness and tried to thank her; but when I opened my mouth to speak, the voice of someone else came out.

The morning's healings moved at what seemed an unnaturally fast pace. Before long, the Geek was at the front, and I had a sudden and overwhelming premonition of doom. Asephone had cured limps and broken limbs and speech impediments, but my friend was too far gone for even her most extraordinary interventions. His whole being was broken, I thought, because girls of my era were taught to believe any deviation was brokenness; he could never be made normal.

Time shifted into bizarre shapes around me, and I found myself stepping outside of it, the here-and-now falling away, and the Geek's attempted healing flashing by in a fraction of a second. I saw it all very clearly, in its entirety.

I should mention that I'd suffered these omens from a very young age.

My father, perhaps demonstrating some second sight himself, had once snapped that if I didn't get myself under control, I would grow up to be a freak show psychic. These impulses have only grown stronger with time. Nowadays, I can tell someone their future just by touching their hand; the Tarot cards and crystal ball are just props. But never in my life did I again have an intuition as strong as the one I felt that day in the circus tent: the Geek wouldn't survive this.

I wanted to call out for him to stop, but, just as in my nightmare, my lips refused to comply. So it was only my brain that screamed as he stepped up

to the raised platform and stared defiantly into the healer's eyes.

"What ails you?" she asked softly.

"All that I am," he replied.

She nodded, as if she'd already
known, and placed a gentle hand on
his forehead.

I think I screamed out loud then.
I don't remember making a sound,
but I do recall my mother clamping
a hand over my mouth, bending over
and hissing at me to behave. I barely
heeded her. My eyes were glued to the
stage.

The Geek cringed a little at her
touch, and the healer's eyes rolled
back in her head, as I'd seen them do
every time before. Usually it was just

a few seconds before her irises flicked back out and resumed their sharp focus. This time, though, they never did.

The healer started to cough and sputter. Her head was thrown back with enough force to snap her neck. At her sides, her hands twitched like those of a man in the electric chair. Her mouth fell open in a silent gasp, and she collapsed, her body falling straight backwards as if she'd been shot.

The room was undoubtedly in uproar, but I heard nothing. All around, mouths hung in silent screams, jaws stretching to reveal slimy tongues and glittering dental fillings. People pointed and hopped from their chairs, which clattered to the ground behind them or were whisked into the path of the amateur heroes rushing to her aid. Finally, a doctor fought his way through the crowd. He waved bystanders away as he checked her pulse, calmly probing her neck, her wrist, before bobbing his head to confirm what we all expected. *She's dead*, he mouthed, but I was sure it was a shout.

Amid the chaos, I saw the Geek slip out undetected beneath the tent flap.

The police looked for him for days, offering a generous reward for his apprehension. But no one ever turned him in.

How did the authorities lose track of such a distinctive figure? The simple answer is that no one had ever taken a photo of the man, and his bizarre appearance was difficult to condense onto a poster. Dozens of witnesses, including my mother, were brought before a police sketch artist—but everyone's description of him produced a radically different picture.

I'm told that shortly after that, the sketch artist quit and took his drawings on tour in a moderately successful exhibition he called "Images of a Freak." I own several of those pieces, now; they were quite difficult to track down, and I treasure them dearly. But none of them resemble the Geek as I remember him.

Like I said, that's the simple answer. The logical answer. But I suspect the Geek had other means of concealing himself, means that defied logic in the way that my visions defy silence and time. In any case, I never saw him again, though I don't doubt he's fine. Men like him are always fine. There are always circuses, and they always need someone to hose off the ele-phants or bite heads off birds or bark at frightened children to entice them closer.

Author Inspiration

I have an affinity for carnivals, circuses, and funhouses. My parents
were involved in the former Ottawa
SuperEx, and my brother and I spent—
conservatively—hundreds of hours on
the grounds as kids. My first job was
in the SuperEX food court, and I still
find it hard to resist the allure of parking lot midways.

Flashing lights, speakers blaring
classic rock, rides painted like album
covers, fairgrounds always had a fantastical atmosphere. Going on a ride
was like being transported into another
world, becoming for a minute an arc-
tic adventurer, a jungle explorer, or
an ecstatic victim of alien abduction.

Been on a Gravitron lately? I swear they run it faster than they used to. Then there's the people who actually <u>run</u> the midway, who have undoubtedly seen some shit in their years on the road.

Throw your hands up as the ride goes backwards, you'll brush against a million stories.

Alice Cooper's <u>The Last Temptation</u> sets a holy war in an abandoned fairground, its opening track "Sideshow" inviting the listener into a world-consuming carnival of wondrous sites and eternal pleasure. Touching on loss of innocence and the seductiveness of sin, that song and that album recall the most sinister stories of Ray Bradbury, as well as Cooper's own classic collaborations with Vincent Price.

I can thank Alice Cooper for "The Geek," not to mention Bradbury, Tod Browning's <u>Freaks,</u> and probably <u>Pee Wee's Big Adventure</u>.

In the story, an aging fortune teller explains how she was once a young girl lured to a circus sideshow and offered a front row seat for a spiritual battle of wills. Its combatants are the Geek, a figure of joyous chaos, and the Healer, a beautiful woman who wants everything to be peaceful and safe, sanitized, and wholesome. There's no Alice Cooper in her ideal world, no carnivals, no interesting people with rough lives and wild stories.

Re-reading the story, I'm not sure the Geek's such a good guy. But the Healer is far more dangerous.

By the way, the SuperEx no longer exists. On its former grounds you can find chain restaurants, a Whole Foods, and many pleasant places to shop. Make of that what you will.

"Dead Drunk Friends"
by Joe Scipione

I pulled the car around the corner, and Justin reached over and patted my thigh as I drove.

"Don't worry," he said. "We'll find it."

It was dark and raining and felt like we'd been driving forever. The plan was to make it another 200 miles on the first day of the drive, but traffic, construction, and the rain slowed our progress. Instead of stopping at the hotel we'd made reservations at, we were driving along back roads and down one-way streets in the middle of nowhere, looking for The Cooper's Hawk Motel. I was starving and just wanted something to eat, a cold beer, and a place to sleep for a while before we hit the road again and got ourselves back on track. This was not the way I wanted to start our cross-country road trip.

"It says the place is just up here on the right. One mile ahead," Justin stared down at his phone and squinted out the windshield as the wipers swished back and forth in front of us. I slowed the car and joined him looking for some tiny, run-down motel.

I rolled the car forward at an even slower pace—it didn't matter, there was no one else on the road with us.

"There it is," Justin said and pointed out the window. I couldn't see what he was pointing at, but the wipers came across my face once again, and I could see the dim motel sign glowing through the dark. The 'L' was not lit up, so the sign read "Mote," but it got the point across. And more important- ly, it meant I could get out of the car and stop driving for the day.

There was one light on in the sin- gle-story building, and we guessed it was the front office. I pulled the car into the parking spot right by the door, sat there, and looked over at Justin.

"Oh right. I'll go get us a room," he said then hopped out of the car and ran into the office. While he was getting our room, a quick search on my phone told me there was a small bar next to the motel. It had a long driveway and was set back from the road, so we couldn't see it when we pulled in. But it would be the perfect place to get some food and drinks after the stressful drive. He came back a few minutes later with a key in his hand.

"Look at this." He held up the key. "Real keys, no key cards or anything. This place is old school."

"Cool." I nodded and tried to sound excited but wasn't sure I pulled it off. It had been a long day. "There's a bar right here. We can drop our stuff and go eat and get some drinks. It's walking distance."

"Sounds great to me," Justin said. We found our room, dropped off our bags, locked it up, and ran through the rain, up the small hill, and down a paved driveway to the small, stand-alone building. The sign above the door read "The 3 AM Tavern." The parking lot was empty, but it sounded like there were a lot of people inside.

Justin opened the door, and we were met with a nearly full bar. There were groups sitting at the tables that filled most of the area inside the place. At the very back was a long bar with a few TV's above it, but they were all off. Nearly every seat at the bar was full. Every person had either long hair or a shaved head, there was no in-between. And they were all wearing leather or denim. It was not really our kind of place, but the aroma of grilled meat that greeted us when we walked in made me realize there was no way I was leaving without eating something first.

The loud rock music blasted and shook the floor as we began to weave our way through the tables, looking for a place to sit. Most people turned and looked at us when we walked by—at least Justin and I weren't the only ones who realized we were out of place.

In the far corner next to the bar was an open table with two chairs. Justin picked up his pace and got to the table before anyone else did. He pulled out my chair, gave me a kiss, then sat opposite me. There was a paper food menu on the table stuffed between the salt and pepper shakers, with a half-full ashtray sitting beside it. There were only four items on the menu—a cheeseburger, pizza, chicken wings, and french fries. The smell of cooked meat when we stepped in had made the decision for me. I already knew I was getting the burger. We sat for only a few minutes before a woman wearing a denim jacket with the sleeves cut off and pair of ripped jeans came over to us.

"We don't usually get newcomers in here," she said. There was no smile on her face, but she didn't seem angry either.

"We're passing through. Staying at the motel next door. We got a little slowed down from the rain," I said.

The woman nodded. "What'll it be?" The words poured from her mouth. It was clear she'd been working there a while.

"Um, I'll have the burger, medium well, with cheese on it," I said. "And fries, please."

She nodded and looked at Justin.

"Same," he said, "but add a couple orders of chicken wings as well, please. Oh, and two waters and two beers."

"Sure thing," the woman said. "Be about ten minutes for the food. Be right back with the drinks."

She walked away, and Justin leaned across the table. "Not really our kind of place," he whispered, though it was easy to hide what he was saying because of the classic rock guitar blaring from the speakers.

"These people seem to like it here, though. They aren't kicking us out or anything. It's a good place to get dinner and drinks anyway." I looked around as I spoke and noticed the waitress coming back with our drinks.

"Here you go." She dropped the glasses of water on our table then placed the bottles of beer down a little more gently. "Food should be a couple more minutes. I'll be back."

She still didn't smile but still seemed nice. The beer was ice cold and exactly what I needed. We each downed about half our beer in one gulp. It had been a long day.

We sat and looked around the bar, though I tried my best not to make eye contact with anyone. This was so far from the usual place Justin and I would have visited, it was hard not to people-watch. I did my best to do it without drawing too much attention to myself.

It wasn't only the people that were interesting, but the bar itself was kind of neat. On the walls hung lots of different '70s and '80s rock band posters. Aerosmith, Guns N' Roses, Alice Cooper, Led Zeppelin, any band you could think of was there. With the same type of music blaring through the speakers, it was clear these people liked their rock 'n' roll. I couldn't argue with them. I liked some good rock as much as the next girl, but as far as fitting in, I was far from it.

"It's a cool little place, huh?" Justin said, drawing my attention back to him.

"Yeah, it really is," I said as I nod-ded. "We could forget the rest of the trip, stay here for vacation."

"That's an idea." Justin laughed at my joke. He was a good boyfriend like that. "For real though, I bet the food here will be better than anything we have the rest of this trip. These places almost always have good greasy food."

We sat for a minute and looked around, not saying anything. I took a long slow breath, just then feeling the tension sliding away after a stressful day in the car.

"Well, fuck you too," a voice rose over the screaming guitar solo. I turned my attention and saw two men standing across the room, staring at each other. One pulled off his jean jacket and let it drop to the floor.

"Sit the fuck down, you don't want this, Lenny," the other guy said. But Lenny stepped up to him. They were nose-to-nose, and Lenny had his hands on the other guy's chest, ready to push him back.

Everyone else in the bar had heard the commotion too. Most of them stopped what they were doing and looked on just like we were, waiting to see what would happen next. I stood to get a better look.

"Holy shit, bar fight," Justin said. I could tell he was more excited than worried about my safety, but he still stood and got in front of me, putting himself between me and the two men about to go at it. Even though it was across the room, you never knew what would happen.

I watched them push and swear and yell back and forth at each other. Some people were watching—most of them laughing. Others looked then went back to whatever it was they were doing before.

"Oh, here goes Lenny and Cole again," someone said behind me. I turned, and the server was putting the food down on our table. She looked at me and continued. "Don't worry they will be hugging it out by the end of the night, no matter what happens right now. Happens every night."

I laughed. "Oh really?"

"Yup, every night," she said. "If you're hungry, might as well eat while the food's hot. There isn't really much to this other than the dick measuring going on."

She laughed and walked away without giving either man her attention. I looked at the food, and my stomach growled. I decided to pass on watching the possible fight and eat instead.

When I sat, Justin joined me. I explained what the woman had said about the two men fighting every night, and we both decided we were just too hungry to wait.

The food was hot and good. The burger had the right amount of grease and flavor, the fries had the right amount of crispiness.

"I told you this food would be great," Justin said before popping another fry in his mouth.

"We might just be starving, but this is great and just what I needed. This place isn't so bad just diff—" I was interrupted by more shouting.

"Lenny, put the knife down," someone said. I turned back to the two men, and sure enough, Lenny held a knife in front of him and was swiping it at Cole. My heart skipped a beat. This was more than two friends having a disagreement. Then I looked around, and more of the crowd was watching Lenny and Cole, but almost everyone was laughing now. Confused, I looked at Justin—who also was staring at the two men—then at everyone else, wondering who was going to put a stop to this fight.

I saw the server a few tables over. She was watching and laughing, then looked over at me and laughed harder. She came over to me, probably on account of the concern plastered across my face.

"Here comes the best part, sweetie. Don't worry." She managed to get the words out between laughs. I was confused but watched the men.

Lenny swiped at Cole again with the knife. Cole stepped back and to the side, and Lenny lunged forward, missing him. Cole roared with laughter, along with the rest of the people in the bar. This obviously angered Lenny, and he looked around, even madder now than he was a few seconds earlier. Only now he wasn't just mad at Cole, he was mad at everyone who'd laughed at him.

"Shut the fuck up!" he shouted, waving the knife in front of his face, pointing the tip at one person in the crowd then the next. Moving toward them only to have them back up and laugh at him again. Lenny's face reddened, and his grip on the knife tightened.

Lenny screamed. It frightened me, and I yelped then covered my mouth with my hand. Justin stood in front of me again. The waitress just laughed and pointed at Lenny. His face got a darker shade of red, redder than I've ever seen a face turn in my life. Was it anger? Embarrassment? Or some combination of the two? At the time, I didn't know.

But it didn't matter.

Lenny struck again with the blade, but unlike the other times, Cole was too slow, and Lenny made contact. At first, I didn't think he'd cut him, but Cole stepped back and put his hands to his throat. My heart pounded in my chest. I wanted to get out of there but was frozen in place. I couldn't tear my eyes from the action—the murder—I was witnessing. Everyone in the bar—except Lenny, Cole, Justin, and I—roared with laughter.

Cole pulled his hands away, and I was expecting to see a spurt of dark crimson flowing down the front of his shirt. There was nothing there. Had it all been a trick? Something to mess with the two newcomers who'd just come in after a long day of driving in heavy rain? I was pissed that they would do this to us.

Then everything changed.

Cole stood motionless and stared at Lenny. He wobbled one way, then the other, teetering on the brink of falling over. Each time I thought he was about to hit the floor, he leaned back the other way. Then he turned his body so he was almost facing me dead-on. His eyes were milky-white, lifeless. His face gray and sunken. There was a long gash on his neck almost like a second smile. His head tipped back, and the crowd watching got quiet. A low murmur went through the bar, as if in anticipation. It got louder as his head went back further and finally fell off his neck. It hit the floor with a thump, and the entire population of the bar roared with applause. Cole still stood there facing me, but his head began to roll toward Lenny.

My hands shook. I wanted to scream but was still frozen, thinking it must be some sort of show. I wanted to reach for Justin—just a few steps in front of me—but I couldn't even lift my arms.

Cole's head continued to roll until Lenny lifted his foot and stopped the thing like a soccer ball. He bent and picked the head up, held it above his head, and the crowd roared once again.

The eyes on the head were closed, the face lifeless, but the entire tavern was captivated by it. After the roar when Lenny held the head aloft, the whole place went still. I wanted to leave and even reached out to tug on Justin's shirt to get him to come with me. We could sneak out the door while everyone else was distracted. I didn't get the chance to pull on his shirt though. My eyes were still glued to the head Lenny held above his own. As were everyone else's in the place.

The eyes on the head—Cole's head—opened. Then his mouth gaped, and he screamed, a huge smile across his face. The crowd erupted once more in laughter. I screamed but was drowned out by the cheering around me. Even Lenny—still holding the head—was laughing and joking. I shook, my hand finally grabbing Justin's shirt, but I didn't know what to do. I gathered myself enough to get Justin's attention, and he turned.

"We need to go!" I shouted over the crowd. He nodded at me and went to grab his wallet from his pocket so he could leave some money on the table. Before he could get it out though, the waitress was there next to us, gripping his arm and looking at him then me.

"Sorry, hun. You gotta stay now until closing. This is the Three AM Tavern, and you can guess what time we close, right?"

I nodded. I felt the tears of fear welling in my eyes, but I didn't want her—or anyone else there—to see how scared I was, so I held them off. I took my seat and pushed the plate of food away. There was no way I could eat after what I'd just watched.

The crowd was now passing Cole's head around and singing some '80s rock song I didn't recognize. Even Cole was singing the song, though his body was still lying in a crumpled mass on the floor next to Lenny. Eventually the head made it to our table. A drunk older woman stumbled by, then stopped and held out Cole's head to us, as if we should join in the festivities and take Cole's head for a lap around the place. I looked at her and shook my head.

"No thanks," Justin said. His voice was quiet, his skin pale. I presumed I looked the same.

"Take him," the drunk woman slurred. She bumped into our table and dropped Cole's head. It came to rest on top of the remnants of my hamburger. His surprisingly animated face smiled up at me.

"Sorry, Cole," the woman said, and she stumbled away. I could feel the eyes of every person in the tavern looking at us—at me. What the hell was going on in this place? I looked away from the bodyless head.

"Hey, hey. Little help here," Cole said from the middle of the plate, the half-eaten burger where his neck should have been.

I looked away, my hands shaking. I wanted to scream but managed to hold it together.

"Please take this," Justin said to anyone who could hear him. A few people around us looked at him. Most, however, turned away, purposely avoiding eye contact with us.

"Hey, hey," Cole's head said again. His eyes shifted to look at Justin, though I'm not sure how much of him Cole could see. "I'm right here. I'm a person. Just take me over to my body, and I'll be fine. Come on. It's not that heavy. Drunk Debbie just held me above her head, and she can barely stand up. Just take me over to my body. Please."

His eyes were strained, and he was begging, pleading with Justin to take him over. If Justin had a flaw, it was that he was too nice. He was even too nice to heads, apparently, because if he was going to touch that fucking thing, the proper course of action was push it off our table and onto the floor. Let someone else deal with it. But he didn't. He sucked in a deep breath, pulled the sleeves of his jacket down over his hands and picked the head up. The crowd cheered and turned their attention to us—to Justin—as he carried Cole's head back to his body.

"Thank you, thank you, thank you," Cole shouted as they walked across the tavern.

The crowd parted around Justin, giving him a path to Cole's body at the other end of the bar. When he stopped, Justin looked down at the head in his hands. The head said something to him, I saw the mouth moving, but I had no idea what it was. Justin's eyes went wide, and he looked back at me and mouthed the word "sorry."

My heart raced. I wanted to run to Justin so he could explain it to me, but I also wanted to run for the door while the entire place was once again distracted by Cole's head. In the end, I did what I'd been doing the whole time, standing and watching, frozen in place. Justin bent and placed the head next to the body, then he took two large steps backward.

What I saw next seemed unreal in the moment and finally shook me from my frozen stupor.

The neck area of Cole's lifeless body began to shimmer and twitch, the greyish pink skin and flesh turned red as if life were returning to it. Millions of tiny tendrils reached out from the neck toward the head, and I noticed the same tendrils writhing and growing out of the bottom of Cole's head. The crowd stood and watched then erupted in another cheer when the tendrils met, became solid, and eventually stopped moving. Cole stood up, turned his head left and right, and threw his hands in the air in celebration. The tavern exploded once more.

I screamed. Justin came toward me, but I was already heading to the door.

"Hey, hey stop her," a voice said from behind me. I ignored it, pushing my way past people who were paying me little to no attention.

"Kelly," Justin called out, but I didn't care. I had to get out of there, and if he wanted to come with me, that was fine, but I wasn't waiting for him. I had to leave.

I got to the door and pushed. The storm outside had gotten worse, and the wind pushed the door back at me. It only opened a crack before it slammed closed on me.

"Kelly, wait!" Justin shouted. I looked back and pushed on the door again, harder.

"Come on!" I leaned against the door, and it flung open just as Justin got to me. He took my hand—the same way he'd always done. Usually I would have turned back to him, but I just wanted to leave, so I tried to get away and out of there.

I felt a tearing in my shoulder. He wasn't pulling me that hard, it was more about my movement away from him. I pulled with all my strength against his hand to get him to let go. He loved me, and I knew he would let me leave if I wanted to. But the tearing sound was louder. There was no pain, just the sound of ripping. I thought it must have been my shirt.

It wasn't.

"Kelly!" he shouted. The wind outside whipped my hair back and forth in my face. I could hear the concern in his voice, so I turned and looked at him. He was a couple steps away from me now. I held the door open with my hip and stared back at him, confused. There was something in his arms, cradled against him.

"Come on," I said. I reached my hand out to take his so we could leave this nightmare place. Screw the motel, we could just get in the car and drive until morning. Anything to get out of there. But when I looked down, there was no hand there. No arm. Justin lifted the thing he was holding, and I realized what it was. He had tears in his eyes as he presented my arm to me.

I collapsed to the ground, half in and half out of the tavern. I felt my shoulder where my arm should have been. There was no pain. There was no blood. There was nothing there. Just the absence of an arm.

"What? What?" I stammered, unable to get a coherent sentence out. Justin knelt on the floor next to me. He held me against his chest—like he'd done so many times before. This time though, I didn't want to be near him, but my body wouldn't work right either.

"This happens to people when they come here. The guy—the head guy— he told me. You come in, you eat and you drink. Then you die. There's nothing you can do about it. We're stuck here, Kel. We're stuck here forever.

We can't leave this place." Justin held out my arm to me, pushing it against my gray, lifeless stump of a shoulder. There was a strange tingling sensation, and within seconds my arm had reattached.

I wiggled my fingers, looked at Justin, and stood. I was already halfway out. I held the door open with the arm that had always been attached to my body and tried to take a step forward. The wind blew hard against the door, and it slammed shut on my left foot. There was a soft crunching sound. The door had taken my foot off when it closed.

Justin helped me back, and I sat on the floor. Someone retrieved my foot for me, and it reattached without any problem. I was dead. So was everyone else in The 3AM Tavern, and there was nothing we could do about it, so I decided to make the best of it.

Years later—I still looked young because you can't age when you're dead—I was sitting at the bar, watching Cole and Lenny go at it for the fifth night in a row, when a young couple entered the tavern. It was snowing outside, and they looked exhausted. I smiled. They'd be able to get rest now with me and all my dead, drunk friends.

Author Inspiration

As a big fan of classic rock music, when I saw there was an anthology taking inspiration from the music of Alice Cooper, I knew it was something I wanted to be a part of. Music plays a huge part in my writing, and I always find myself brainstorming and getting ready to write by listening to music that I think fits with the mood of what I am writing at that moment. If you're ever reading any of my books, chances are I have a Spotify playlist I listened to while getting ready to write.

The song that was the inspiration for this story is the song "My Dead Drunk Friends" by the Hollywood Vampires—

Alice's collaboration with Joe Perry of Aerosmith and Johnny Depp. I remember the first time I heard this song on the Hollywood Vampires first album. I thought then that the song would do great as a music video or even in a movie, because you could hear not just the band, but an entire barroom full of "dead, drunk, friends." I love the hook on this song and find it really catchy, and it is something I want to listen to a few times in a row.

When I sat down to write this story, I wanted to know more about the people in the bar and how they got there. Once I started in that direction, the story came pretty quickly. I wanted the story to have the same over-the-top ridiculousness that I feel the song features, and I think it accomplishes that pretty well. This story was a blast to write, and I hope you had a grin on your face while reading it, because I was smiling the whole time I was writing.

"A Dress to Die For"
by Petina Strohmer

Opening the door releases a swarm of flies.

The room is dark, damp, and stinks of decay.

Taking a deep breath, the cop covers his mouth with his hand and turns on the light.

How do you get bloodstains out of silk?

I run my fingers over the marks on my wedding dress. The fresher ones are still red. The older ones have faded to black.

Does it matter how long they've been there?

A whole history of pain, revenge, and death spread across the sheer material.

What if the blood belongs to more than one person?

To be honest, it's a moot point. I'm never taking this dress off. Not now. Not ever. I think everybody understands that ... at last.

Mile after mile after mile.

Rumbling along the endless, empty asphalt, I figure out how to drive my truck in my attire. The voluminous folds of the skirt aren't as much of a problem as operating the pedals in sparkly high heels. I really want to wear the veil down, but the visibility is just too poor. Still, a girl can't always get exactly what she wants—even on her big day.

The bodice is a bit tight, but it does wonders for the cleavage, and the garter is chafing the inside of my thigh. Sometimes you just have to suffer for the sake of beauty. And every time I turn the steering wheel, I just love the jangly sounds from the multitude of silver bracelets around my wrists.

It's been a long day, and as the sunset streaks across the horizon like an open wound, I realise I'm getting tired and hungry, and I need a break. As if by magic, the golden arches appear. God bless Maccies.

The rig crunches to a halt in the parking lot, its air brakes hissing, and I have to work out how to get out of the cab in this dress. I have to be careful, because I don't want to get it covered in oil; the bloodstains are bad enough.

The only customer in the place at this hour, I order my food and try to ignore the surreptitious stares of the staff. Still, I can't blame them. I *am* gorgeous.

Trying to decide whether I want fries or carrot sticks with my burger—a girl's got to watch her weight—I hear the door open and close but don't turn round. Urgent mutterings sound behind me until somebody reaches past my long black hair, braided with pearls, and taps on my shoulder. "Are you okay, ma'am? I couldn't help noticing the blood on your dress."

"Why, thank you," I say, turning to give the biker my best smile, "but I'm just fine."

His stubbled jaw falls open, and his eyes almost pop out of his head. "What the …" His companions seem similarly surprised, no doubt stunned by my beauty.

"Now now, boys," I chide them. "Don't you know it's rude to gawp at a lady?"

I don't see the first blow coming, but I feel my nose fracture from the force of the fist. A storm of blood bursts from the middle of my face and joins the rest on my soiled dress. Before I can react, a swift uppercut snaps my head back, blood flying in a scarlet arc.

The staff begin screaming and shouting. One gallant young man even jumps over the counter to come to my aid. But this girl knows how to handle herself. Still sticky from its last outing, I grab the razor sharp knife hidden in my garter, and the next hand that comes my way loses three fingers.

Chaos ensues. In a chorus of howls and curses, fists and feet fly; blades slash, slice, and stab; and the whole restaurant is redecorated in red. By the time the police sirens join the cacophony, I'm the last one standing. I bet they weren't expecting to see that!

※ ※ ※

It wasn't murder, it was self-defence, but try telling that to the judge. Perhaps it was my attire that confused him.

I'll admit that my beautiful dress ain't quite so beautiful now. It's ripped and torn. Damp and dirty and, to be honest, it's starting to stink. In addition to the stains it already had, it's now covered in my blood, that of the bikers, and the prison guards who tried to take it off me. Like I was going to swap silk for a denim jumpsuit. Anyway, orange is *so* not my colour. I did warn them, but I guess they thought this one little girl was no match for them. They know different now.

Pinning me to the floor, one was actually laughing in my face while the other had his hands up my skirt. They were calling me "darling" and "sweetheart" and saying how they were going to punish me for being such a naughty girl.

I waited until I could smell cheap cologne and feel whiskers against my chin, then I whipped out my hand and stuck my painted fingernails into one guard's eye. As he lurched backwards, the eyeball was ripped from the socket, bouncing about on his cheek as he writhed and screamed. Before his partner could react, I leapt forward and sank my teeth into his face. The harder he tried to push me away, the deeper I bit, until I spat what was left of his nose onto the cell floor.

Somehow this act of self-defence was also added to my list of offences

... but nobody ever tried to undress me again.

Prison life isn't so bad, especially in the company of all these men. And what do you know, most of the inmates are more understanding and accepting of me than the outside world ever was.

There are a few nasty bastards (well, it is prison), but the jibes and threats stopped when I became Big Billy's gal. The biggest, baddest con is feared and respected by all the other men, prisoners and guards alike. I don't know if he'd heard the details of that night in the burger joint and was impressed at what a sassy little lady I am, or perhaps it's simply my feminine charm.

Only I know he has a hidden heart, a secret softer side. It just took a good woman to find it.

Most inmates have physically demanding jobs; some swelter all day in the laundry, others toil in the workshop, and the toughest of all are on the chain gang. Of course, none of this is suitable employment for a lady. I'm not about to break my nails busting rocks, so Billy has ensured that I look after the library instead.

Such a sweet boy.

All in all, my life in jail is settled and comfortable.

Then they found my sister.

I turned the key and stepped over the threshold. I'd stood on the tatty doormat so often over the years, but that day was the first time in a long time.

One whiff of the musty air, and I was transported back forty years. The floral wallpaper, faded lino, and big pine kitchen table remained. Missing was the slender, aproned figure, singing softly to herself as she stirred the cooking pot, adding a pinch of this and a peck of that until a meal of cheap meat tasted like a banquet.

Running my fingers across the chop-
ping board, the old ruts and gashes
told its history like Braille. One story
was when I returned from my first
fishing trip and proudly presented the
tiniest trout. My dad and my sister,
Suzie, both laughed, but Mom received
and prepared the little fish as if it were
a huge salmon.

Tears fractured my vision. She was
perfect—beautiful, funny, and kind. I
could never be half the woman she
was, and I didn't know what I was going to do without her.

Dad died when we were still
young. Bitten to the bone by can-
cer, Adonis became Methuselah; thin
skin stretched over sharp bones, his

mouth full of ulcers, and his eyes full of tears. My devoted mother nursed him all the way through his decline while still comforting and caring for two bewildered children. Thanks to her, my father was able to die at home surrounded by love.

After he was gone, money was tight, so Mom channelled her grief into hard work. She took on two jobs to keep a roof over our heads but still managed to be home when my sister and I returned from school.

We never, ever saw her cry.

She loved this house. Full of memories of her family, it was almost a part of her, and she stayed as long as she could. Dementia is a cruel disease.

Slowly and silently, it sucked the life out of our mother, leaving no more than a frail and fragile husk. The staff of the nursing home were kind and considerate and provided the round-the-clock care she now needed, but the day Mom no longer recognised her children was the day she died.

Her decrepit body hung onto life for years afterwards; her heart pumped, her lungs drew ragged breath, but looking into her eyes, we could tell she had left the building. Of course, we continued to visit the hollow shell that used to be her, but we couldn't bring ourselves to sell her house, the home to which she'd never return, until she finally gave up the ghost. Borrowing against the property to pay the nursing home bills meant the place was finally up for sale.

My sister and I arranged to meet at the house one last time to sort out Mom's things.

Despite growing up in a home full of love, Suzie and I were never friends. Mom wouldn't dream of playing favourites, but it didn't stop my sister from trying. She took the credit for anything good and blamed the rest on me.

One of the things I loved most about Mom was that she accepted and loved me unconditionally. She understood the way I was. Though Suzie would never dare bully me at home, she and her horrible friends hounded me mercilessly everywhere else. At school, in the park, at the mall. The only place I ever felt safe was by Mom's side. She was forever asking me what was wrong, but I wouldn't say; not to protect my spiteful sister but to spare my poor Mom the pain.

Suzie and I grew up, but nothing really changed.

And there she was, parading around in our mother's wedding gown. I loved everything about that dress; the colour, the cut, the feel of silk on skin. Sometimes, when Dad and Suzie were out, Mom would let me try it on. I clonked round the bedroom in oversized shoes with the sparkly tiara falling over my eyes and with armfuls of ivory lace. If we had time, Mom would let me put on a little of her mascara, a swipe of scarlet lipstick, and I felt like the belle of the ball. We would laugh and dance together, and she always told me that one day, the divine dress would be mine.

There was no way in hell I was going to let Suzie rob me of that.

"Take it off," I growled.

She continued to swirl in front of the mirror.

"Take. It. Off. It's mine."

"You've gotta be kidding me," she laughed, admiring her reflection.

"Do I look like I'm joking?"

She ignored me. The hooped skirt swirled around her slim hips as she turned, the light sparkling off every sequin. Her body filled the silk bodice perfectly, and the veiled headdress swathed her head like a gossamer crown.

The dress did look good on Suzie but ...

"I'm the older child, so it's mine, that's what Mom said," I reminded her.

She gathered up the folds of soft material. "And what are you going to do with it?"

"Dur—wear it?"

Her shrieks of merriment grated on my nerves. "On your big day? Or are you planning to wear it to Walmart?"

"I'll do what I like with it—because it's mine."

Suzie stopped dancing and fixed me with those bright blue eyes. "Listen Ali, Mom might have pandered to your ... delusions, but she's gone now. It was her dress, passed down from her mother, and next spring," she patted down the lace panels, "I'll be getting married in it."

"But it's mine."

She rolled her eyes. "It's time to grow up and live in the real world now. This exquisite creation would be wasted on you and whatever weird things you intend to do in it." She shuddered. "It's a wedding dress, designed to be worn at a wedding, and that's exactly what's going to happen."

"Take it off," I said again.

"What? No!"

"Take the dress off." I felt my hackles rising.

"Or what?" She pouted her painted lips. "Is little Ali going to throw a big baby tantrum? Roll around the floor and scream until you're sick? It might have worked on Mom, but it won't work on me. I loved that woman with all my heart, but she was way too soft on you. Indulging all your weird little fantasies as a child has just made you a really weird adult. Dad would never have—"

Her hysterical diatribe was halted by a punch in the mouth. By the time she came around, the sparkling slipper was on the other foot.

"Wha—whas going on?" she slurred, squinting at the rope that held her hands above her head. "What are you doing, you psycho?"

"Just taking back what's mine," I told her, checking the tension on the ties.

"What?"

"It's my dress," I reminded her calmly, "and I'm taking it."

Her bruised face contorted into an ugly sneer. "Over my dead body."

"If need be."

"Yeah, right," she scoffed until I held up the knife.

Her smile disappeared. "Seriously?"

My sister and I were alike in many ways. She might have been scared, but I knew that wasn't going to silence her sass. I wasn't expecting this to be easy, but I had come prepared.

"Whatcha gonna do, Ali Cat?" She knew I hated her calling me that. "Cut it off me?"

"I'd rather not damage the dress unless I have to." My tone was calm, controlled, but that wasn't fooling her.

"You've finally flipped, haven't you?" she sneered. "Everyone always said you were a nut job."

"Shut up."

"Even Mom."

"I said, shut up."

"Just not to your face."

"Shut up!" I lunged forward and a scarlet slice appeared in the arm of her dress.

"Whoa!" Suzie was surprised, but, like me, she was empowered by pain. "Cuz that's really the action of a sane person."

Blood ran down her arm and dripped onto the cream carpet. I stared at the steadily spreading stain.

"You like that?" she leered. "Is that what gets you off, Ali Cat?"

The second swipe cut across her chest. But she was still laughing. "You're a complete loony tune," she spat. "A real wonky weirdo. I tried to protect you, Mom tried to protect you, but everybody knows it—including you."

There was red on the dress, on the carpet, and in the rage that rose before my eyes. I lunged at my sister again.

Cutting carefully, I removed the dress from Suzie's body. Her throat bled profusely, and she could no longer speak, but she was still breathing. I had made sure of that.

"I did warn you," I chided her. "Wouldn't it have been easier to take it off when I first asked you?"

A gurgling noise bubbled from her in response.

"Let's just say, for argument's sake, I *was* insane." I continued to cut. "Was the wisest course of action to enrage me?"

One of the straps caught on her shoulder. I sliced through the flesh to free it. She groaned.

"You say I'm a psycho—oh." The bottom of the zipper was stuck. Gouging into the small of Suzie's back released it. Another strangled moan.

"Then you're surprised if I act like one?"

The edge of the veil was attached to a ring on my sister's finger. To be fair,

I did try to ease it off first. The bloody digit fell to the floor.

One final slice down the side and the dress fell away from her sodden body leaving a long gash that exposed the shiny muscle beneath. She sagged as the last of her life drained away.

I studied her lacerated corpse, still spinning gently on the rope. Though now stained with blood, the precious dress was intact, courtesy of the numerous slices and slashes all over Suzie's body. Holding the fabric to my face, I inhaled deeply, smearing blood all across my chin. "A dress to die for." I smiled.

I don't like this place.

After the authorities found Suzie's body, they moved me out of prison and into here. They said it was for everyone's safety, but I don't see how.

Everything here is just so … strange. It's all white; walls, ceiling, floor, even the uniforms of the staff who creep up and down the corridors in soft shoes.

And everywhere is so quiet. The T.V. is turned down too low, meals are eaten in silence, and if anyone talks at all, it's only in infuriating whispers. Occasionally, the peace is perforated by a scream, usually at night, but Matron, wielding her sharp syringe, soon puts a stop to that.

The inmates here don't really communicate with each other, seemingly locked in their own little worlds. It's a far cry from the sociable hustle and bustle of Billy's place. I hope they send me back soon. My man must be so lonely without me, and if I'm stuck in this weird ward for much longer, I'm gonna go mad.

The straitjacket is made of coarse cotton which does not go well with silk but underneath, I can still feel my mother's dress against my skin. Nobody's ever going to take that away from me. Not now. Not ever.

Clicking his fingers to get my attention, the psychiatrist stares into my eyes. "Mr Cooper," he says in that maddeningly gentle voice. "Do you understand why you're here?"

But I'm not here. I'm a million miles away. At a wedding. My wedding. And don't I make the perfect bride.

"Mr Cooper," he tries again. "Do you have any questions?"

Slowly he comes back into focus.

"Just one," I say. "How do you get bloodstains out of silk?"

Author Inspiration

I have loved Alice Cooper since I first saw him on the 1982 *Special Forces* tour, and he remains my favourite live artist. "The Saga of Jesse Jane" from the <u>Dirty Diamonds</u> album of 2005, always makes me smile, but, as a writer, I wondered both about the character's backstory and what might happen to him in the future.

The result is "A Dress to Die For." Enjoy!

"Daddy-Daughter Dance"
by Bert Edens

I wish I'd killed my ex-wife. I mean, she's still fucking dead. But I wish I'd been the one to send her to whatever Circle of Hell that Dante would have picked. No doubt, she'd have been a good candidate for any of them.

Not that I regret the time we spent together, because I did get my darling Betty out of it. It's the only consolation I have these days. And the only positive I have from our marriage.

Like most relationships, it started all hot and heavy, but it cooled over time. I was sitting in a nearly empty theater watching some forgettable mid-2010s horror flick when Rosie plopped down next to me unannounced and inter- twined our arms for the last half of the movie. Sometimes her nails dug into my palm or arm so deep, I thought she was going to bring blood. But the scent of her blond hair, a mix of vanilla and raspberry, carried me through the pain, and I felt more than a little stir- ring between my legs now and again.

We banged that night and several nights in a row after that. We were pretty much inseparable right away.

Six months later we got hitched. Ten months later Betty came along.

Yeah, your math is right. Didn't please Rosie's parents too much, knowing their daughter got knocked up outside wedlock, but Betty's sparkling blue eyes and blond hair, which matched her mom's, won them over. Grandbabies are grandbabies after all. And I gotta admit, she'd melt my heart when her whole hand would squeeze my pinkie and she'd gaze at me. Almost made cleaning the toxic waste that ended up in her diaper worth it. Almost.

Being the dutiful geeky husband and father I was, or least thought I wanted to be, I buried myself in my work to try and provide for my family. The good thing about doing web design is you can do it from damn near any-where at any time of the day. As long as you got an internet connection to update sites when you're ready, you're good to go. I could be dropped down in the middle of fucking Siberia, and I could work, as long as I could hit a coffee shop with wi-fi once in a while.

Not that we lived in Siberia, but we might as well have, living in the mid-dle of the Ozark Mountains of Arkan-sas. I spent a shit-ton to get internet run to our house, but it paid off. I could work night and day, plugging away at paying the bills.

As the cliché goes, I buried myself in my work and lost sight of everything going on around me. That's what happens when you're so fucking deep you can't see out of the hole you created. And what I failed to see was that Rosie had taken a shine to one of the neighbor's boys. I say boy, but he was like 25 or so. Oh sure, she said she was running to town or going to see her Grandma Ethel, but you can't hide from a geek, we're too damn smart. It was easy enough to slip an Air Tag into the lining of her purse, and I could track her anywhere.

And that anywhere always ended up being at Vince Potter's house, where he lived with his old man after his momma kicked the bucket a few years back. Just the two of them. Of course, we knew the Potters, hell everyone knew everyone around here, and fucking half of everyone was kin. That also made it easy to tell when that Air Tag came to rest on Vince's end of their house, where my 'Til Death Do Us Part was getting her field plowed by that farmer boy.

Eventually, I confronted her about it, but she was no idiot. She knew what leverage to use to get me to stay, or at least not kick her ass out. Yeah, no surprise, it was that ten-month-old darling daughter of mine. She was daddy's girl, although not really a Daddy's Girl. The threat of never seeing her again kept me around, even though I started sleeping on the couch. I couldn't share a bed with a bitch whose body I knew someone else was enjoying instead of me.

We lived like that for a year or so, the tension constant and oppressive, at least to me. I tight-roped like a circus performer, trying to make Rosie happy so she'd keep herself and Betty around, while she spent a bunch of her time at Vince's funhouse. That didn't mean we didn't argue, because we certainly did. And one time, as I was bitching at her, she screamed back, "What are you gonna do about it?"

So I showed her. I had slapped her before I realized it, but on the backswing, my hand was closed, knocking two teeth loose, which skittered across the floor and under the coffee table, leaving bloody paths like rocks skipped on the lake.

I knew I should have apologized, but I couldn't. Fuck her. This was all her fault. She'd poked the bear one too many times and finally paid the price.

I wasn't surprised by the divorce papers. But I was surprised by the jail time for assault. Only thirty days, and in this Podunk county seat, I was the only one there most of the time, other than when it became the occasional overnight drunk tank.

Naturally, Rosie got damn near everything, thanks to the asshole judge who had played high school football with her daddy. I did at least get to keep my 2007 POS Honda Civic and my laptop, so I could keep making a living, so that's something.

I ended up parking outside Norris Insurance on the downtown square to do my work. That idiot had no idea what secured wi-fi was, so I could leech off him for internet access. When nights came around, I couldn't very well sleep in my car since the jail was literally in the courthouse behind me. So I'd park on some side road off one of the countless dirt roads, trying to keep moving around so nobody would complain.

It's amazing how long you can keep up something like that, but I couldn't afford a place because of how much that fucking judge had set the child support at. Every penny I made went toward food, gas, or Rosie. Of course, she wouldn't make her and Vince official since that would stop her gravy train from me, even though I knew they were both shacked up in my old house.

So, from the time the bitch made me hit her until things turned around, a little over two years passed. Betty was getting bigger, I guess, since I was never invited over for birthday parties or anything. And I couldn't spend time with her because I was a "violent offender."

Then my grandma, my mom's mom, took a dirt nap and left me her house just up from the dam on Beaver Lake. Fortunately, her will hadn't been updated in years, so it never mentioned Rosie or Betty. So it was all mine, free and clear. All I had to come up with were property taxes and utilities. That I could manage, since I didn't need to drive anywhere anymore. Hell, with grocery delivery, I didn't even need to leave for that.

Of course, Rosie disputed the will, but that actually went my way. So I kept to myself for the most part, other than the odd runs to town. I did spend some time parked outside Rosie's house, eyeballing through the windows all the goings on. Once in a while I'd catch a glimpse of Betty, or at least the top of her head, through a window. There was one time I saw Vince tossing her up in the air and catching her, and it made me want to kick in the front door and break his fucking face. That's my baby girl, not his. How dare he.

One of the good things about doing websites is you tend to do the same ones over and over, with just names and images changing. You could have a template that saved a ton of work. That made work a lot faster, so I could get more jobs. I was eventually able to cut the cable internet cord and get satellite internet, which was a hell of a lot faster. Well, once I got the dish to the top of that monster pine behind the house.

I'm not sure when it started happening, but I started making mistakes. Clients would bitch about me misspelling their names or some piddly shit like that. Yeah yeah yeah, customer's always right and all that. But they seemed to be making up problems too. I know I'm human after all. Shit, I'd lost track of the times Rosie had told me I was a fuck-up. But I knew I wasn't making that many mistakes.

One client made up some bullshit excuse about missed deadlines and canceled on me, claiming breach of contract. Fuckers. That cost me three grand. Fortunately, I was taking the Wal-Mart method of business, doing a shit-ton of jobs for less, so it didn't hurt too bad. But it still stung the old bank account.

There were times at home I'd swear I heard Betty laugh. I'd run through the house trying to find her, but she always seemed to be one room ahead of me. Eventually, it would fade away, and I'd run outside and look for her. But she wasn't there anymore. I figured Rosie was just screwing around with me, because that was just like her.

I've always been one who loved to be part of nature. I could sit my ass on a Caribbean beach or along an Ozarks stream or even on some log in the middle of the forest, and I'd be perfectly happy. Fortunately, the forest around my house had a lot to explore and more than a few trails. So I liked to wander around and clear my head, especially when the clients started thinning out. I figure I was probably getting undercut by some assholes in India or something, which was hard to compete with. I didn't have a lot of bills, but I still had enough, especially trying to keep up with that damned child support.

On one of those walkabouts, I was just about to cross back over County Road 69 to head back down the hill to my house, when I saw a car upside down on the side of the road. Kinda looked like that new Corolla I'd seen Rosie driving around town, which had only pissed me off more, knowing my money was going to her and not my baby girl.

I approached the car and could smell gas and that noxious chemical odor antifreeze makes when it hits a hot engine block. Steam rose from the front, where the car had hit a massive oak. As I got closer, I could see a woman next to the tree. It looked like she'd been a javelin through the front window, and where she'd skidded across the ground, her pale blue sweater had been pulled down, exposing a tit.

She wasn't moving, and I knew I should call 911, even though signals sucked out here. But I rolled her over to get a better look. The right side of her face looked like she'd lost a fight with a cheese grater. Flesh and muscle flapped around as I moved her, exposing teeth and a tongue that lolled through the gap in her cheek. A crimson streak across the bark of the oak said everything.

But what I could see of her face was definitely Rosie. She'd dyed that gorgeous blond hair of hers black, and she'd obviously had a boob job, because I'd always told her she'd make a lousy tit fuck. But it was definitely her. I grabbed a handful of the exposed breast. Yep, definitely silicone. More shit my child support had gone to that it shouldn't have.

I left her there and went to the back of the car, certain my Betty would be there. And she was, looking bigger than I'd remembered, so at least she'd been eating well. Rosie had also dyed Betty's hair black, which I thought you shouldn't do with kids because of all the chemicals and how it would damage their locks. But apparently, that hadn't mattered to Rosie.

In typical Irresponsible Rosie fashion, Betty wasn't wearing her seat belt. Her body had crumpled against the roof, her head at such an odd angle that her ear was against her shoulder. Dull brown eyes stared back at me, unblinking. At least she was wearing a burgundy dress, the same color we had always put her in.

Pulling Betty from the car, I cradled her in my arms, careful to support her head, and began the two-mile trek through the woods back to my house. By the time we got home, I was sweating profusely, even though it was winter. I walked a lot, but I wasn't used to the extra 50 pounds I had been lugging.

The good thing about Grandpa, who'd died more than ten years ago, and Grandma was, they had a second bedroom, just in case any grandkids or great-grandkids ever came over to stay. Not that they did, but at least the space was there.

Grandma had done up the room right, with a nice queen bed and fluffy comforter. Two monster pillows filled the bed, the pillow slips all roses and lace. A chest-of-drawers stood in the corner in place of a closet. The ceiling fan desperately needed cleaning, and as I laid Betty on the comforter, I made a note to do so. Fortunately, she didn't appear to be bleeding, so I didn't worry about her making a mess on the bed.

I sat on the couch and pondered for a bit. I'd never considered how I would manage being a single parent. I'd only every considered Rosie and I with Betty or me without Betty at all. Yet, there my baby girl was in the spare bedroom. And I didn't have to share her with anyone, now that the wicked witch was dead. *Ding Dong*, indeed.

That night as I watched the news, I saw a story about some lady named Maria who'd died in a car crash not far from me. Her daughter had apparently wandered off into the woods trying to find her way home, because she wasn't in the car. That would fuck me up if that had happened to my Betty. The next morning, some volunteers stopped by my house to see if I'd seen the girl, but Betty and I hadn't gone anywhere, so I didn't have anything to tell them.

Of course, I wanted to keep Betty forever, so I learned how to rewire the air conditioning so her room was on its own thermostat. Again, it's good to be a geek. I tried to keep her room about 40 degrees or so. I even blacked out her windows so the heat from the sun wouldn't raise the temp.

As a lover of music, I have a massive vinyl collection. I pretty much always have something spinning when

I'm home, unless I'm watching TV. But the album I love the most is Judy Collins's *Who Knows Where the Time Goes*. Betty and I especially love the opening track, "Hello Hooray," which is amazing but was butchered when it was covered by some forgettable seventies rock band. I love holding Betty close to me as we slow dance around the living room.

Despite her cold room, Betty's body did start breaking down a bit. When I saw her belly swelling, I found a basting needle in the kitchen and used that to release the gas buildup. Had to do that with her chest too. Man, that stench was nasty, so I put out several vanilla candles in her room and kept them lit all the time.

Since we love dancing in the living room, I eventually started keeping the temperature in the whole house in the forties. I'd much rather wear a sweater or jacket all the time, as long as that meant my Betty could be with me longer. For an older house, the insulation is amazing, so it's easy to keep the whole house cold.

To keep my Betty's joint supple, I tried almost every day to bend or rotate her wrists, elbows, shoulders, hips, and knees. It certainly made dancing easier and more enjoyable when I could spin her around with me and she didn't feel like a scarecrow.

I couldn't handle it when Betty's eyes became cloudy, so I made another run to town, this time to Hobby Lobby. I found some blue doll's eyes that looked to be around the right size for Betty. After plucking out her old eyes with tweezers and severing the optic nerve, I tried putting the new ones in, but they kept falling back into her head. So I broke out the Gorilla Glue and attached the inside of her lids to the new blue eyes, and that worked like a charm.

But despite my best efforts, her body kept falling apart. The first tear in her flesh I noticed was on the inside of her left elbow. The skin just separated, and I could see where her muscles had pulled away from the bone as they deteriorated. Her ulna and humerus were much whiter than I thought they'd be, although it's not like I had seen many children's bones.

Betty's skin was starting to toughen, almost like leather. So I decided I needed to start putting lotion on her skin to keep it softer. But in the meantime, I had to do something about her elbow. Lucky for me, YouTube is a wonderful place to learn just about anything, and I learned how to do a baseball stitch. I found some of Grandpa's old leather boots in the shed, and I cut them into strips so I'd have something to practice on. A steak knife let me poke small holes I could use to thread a needle through.

Of course, I didn't have the needle and thread I needed just laying around, but a quick trip to Wal-Mart took care of that. Once I felt comfortable enough stitching, pulling apart, and repeating the process, I went to work on Betty, who by then had developed more tears on the outside of one knee and in an armpit. I worried about her getting worse, but I wasn't about to give up our Daddy-Daughter dances.

The regular application of lotion definitely helped, and it made repairs on Betty much easier. I actually nailed all three fixes the first time. But all that did was delay the inevitable. A few days later, as we were whirling around the living room, I spun a little too hard, and her flesh ripped across her throat, the weight of her head tearing all around her neck. Fortunately, while one arm was extended with hers, the other was at the small of her back, allowing me to neatly catch her head as it fell.

That repair took a little longer just because of the magnitude of it. When I was done, I had to confess she was starting to look like Frankenstein's monster. Her hair had started falling out in clumps, and it had taken more Gorilla Glue to reattach it. I had to use a black Sharpie to color spots on her scalp showing through my shitty repair work. But she was still my baby. That's all that mattered.

Now, as Betty snuggles with me on my lap, I watch the news. Some moron let a campfire get out of control over at Dam Site Park, and the whole fucking hillside is on fire. I can smell the smoke blowing our way, so I know it's close. But we are fine, here in our home.

Still we snuggle. I give her kisses on her forehead, rub her back, console her, and repeat over and over how much I love her. When I see branches on the oak tree by our front porch ignite, I lift my Betty, crank up Judy Col-

lins, and begin our final Daddy-Daughter dance.

Author Inspiration

As the editor of this anthology, I intentionally waited until all stories had been submitted and accepted until I wrote mine, because I didn't want to pick a song that someone else had written a story for, even if it hadn't been accepted. My favorite Cooper song is "Dead Babies," but I just couldn't come up with a story that worked without it essentially being a straight retelling of the song.

But one day, I was listening to the song "Billion Dollar Babies," and the phrase where he's talking about dancing with her and worrying about her head falling off stuck with me. The song itself is about the excess of the super-rich, but I wondered, what would happen if this happened, literally losing her head? And what if she were a child? What would lead the narrator to that point? What kinds of things would go sideways to lead him there? And that's the seed that produced this story.

"It's Hot Tonight"
by Melissa M. Dudek

I t's hot tonight."

Captain Obvious felt the need to point this out to me. I felt the need to pretend not to hear.

It was too hot for talking. Especially to coppers.

The clock on the corner said it was after midnight, but it was still roasting. For the last three days, the sun scorched the city in the daytime. The humidity kept it steaming through the night. I hadn't had a wink of shut-eye since Tuesday. That wasn't going to change tonight, but at least this time, it wasn't the heat making me crazy.

If I closed my eyes, I knew I'd see it again. I hadn't blinked in an hour out of fear of seeing it again. Seeing Maurice Escargot's dead body.

On cue, two flatfoots wheeled a gurney out of Paul's Boutique. Escargot had an office above the shop. We had an office above the shop. Or we did before someone cut his head off.

Someone, or something, had just rubbed out my partner.

"You the gumshoe that found him?"

I demoted him to Corporal Obvious. He didn't deserve an officer's stripes.

"Bad business."

I headed down the street away from Private Obvious. Away from it all.

If they needed me, they knew where to find me. My office was upstairs, or it used to be back when Maurice Escargot still had a head.

I walked down the empty avenue. Dogs in the distance were airing their heat-related complaints in high-pitched, continuous barking. Cats' screams echoed through every alleyway. But there were no creatures to be seen. The sound of the paddy wagon rolling in hot had sent all the geezers scampering indoors.

It was even too hot for the road rats.

It wasn't too hot for Angel. Nothing was too anything for Angel. She was one tough broad.

She needed to know what happened, and I needed to tell her. If I could find her. Angel had to want to be found for someone to do so.

If I did find her, what would I tell her? She was a tough cookie, but no one was tough enough for the whole story.

I must have blinked because the scene flashed in my brain. The memory replayed in black and white. Even my brain wasn't tough enough for the whole story, at least not the Technicolor version.

I knew things were crummy the moment I opened the office door. There was a single cigarette in the ashtray. Escargot never smoked only one cigarette or only one pack. There should have been at least two dozen butts there. The empty bottle of Seagram's tracked, but the three fingers of it remaining in the highball didn't. Neat, no rocks was how he liked it, but Escargot would have killed the glass the second he poured it. There was no such thing as leftover rot gut in his world. I recognized his snubnose and bullets, but they were sitting atop a cheap dime store novel. "The outstanding mystery discovery of the decade," the front cover declared. It didn't matter how great it was. Escargot didn't read. Even his torn-out pin-up gal pages needed to be word free.

The black lace bra on the desk was new. That was another reason I needed to find Angel. Maybe I wasn't going to have to paint her a picture. She might be the one filling in the blanks for me. Blanks like how he came to lose his head.

I shook off the memory before the rest of the office could come into focus. Even in black and white, it was too gruesome.

"Hella hot tonight, ain't it?"

Angel was leaning up against a light post five feet ahead. She wore a skintight black dress, cinched in the

middle by a snakeskin belt accentu-
ating her ample curves. Her matching
snakeskin heels gave her long legs an
extra three inches of height.

I took off my fedora and wiped the
sweat from my forehead as I walked
up to her. It was still too hot to talk,
but I had to.

"I heard."

"All of it?"

"Enough."

She pulled out a cigarette. I pulled
out my lighter and did the honors.

"I loved that goofy sonofabitch."

"I know."

I put the lighter back into my pocket. It was even too hot to smoke.

"Did he do it to himself?"

"Doubtful." She clearly hadn't heard all of it, and I wasn't going to tell her.

"Who did it?"

"That's what I'm going to find out. You see him tonight?"

"Haven't seen him since Tuesday."

I suddenly wished it weren't too hot to smoke. I was jonesing for a cigarette, especially knowing the question I had to ask.

"He been stepping out on you?"

She took a long drag. "Talk to Kachina."

Before I could ask where I could find Kachina, she spat out her cigarette, ground it out with her shoe, and walked away.

So Escargot had a side piece? I had to give him credit. I didn't think he had it in him. He was punching well above his weight with Angel. He was no king of the silver screen. He was a tall, lanky souse with a thick, black head of hair that was always tucked into his fedora. It was hard to imagine what she saw in the scruffy, smoky, hard-drinking, hard-staring dick shoved into a cheap suit. Or what this Kachina did as well.

Or what they used to see in him. When he still had a head.

Technically, Escargot did still have a head. It was just no longer attached to his shoulders. His torso was sitting at the desk, arms limp at his sides. His head was on the windowsill, one eye open and one closed. It wasn't the only head on the sill.

I reached into my front pocket and pulled out my cigarettes, shoving one in my mouth and lighting up. It was no longer too hot to smoke.

I headed to Escargot's digs, hoping to beat the coppers to the scene. His place was a walk-up three blocks from the office, a studio on the sixth floor.

It was too hot to walk up six flights of stairs, but with no black and whites in sight, I did just that.

By the time I made it to 6F, my dress shirt was soaked through. I found the key under the mat and let myself in. I headed straight for his closet and grabbed his one clean shirt off the hanger. He wasn't going to be needing it any time soon. His funeral was not going to be open casket.

I decided to go for broke and took his last clean tie. It was loud enough to wake the dead and not my usual style, but if I was going to be interrogating dames, I should be dressed for it.

I looked in the mirror, loosened the tie, and undid the shirt's top button. No broad was worth a fully knotted tie at that time of night or in that heat.

"It's sure hot tonight."

I turned around to find a dishy doll leaning up against the wall. She wore a white blouse unbuttoned to the third closure with tight black pants hugging her lower curves. Bright red fingernails grasped a whiskey glass.

"Kachina?"

She took a sip of her whiskey.

"Bass Levin." I loosened my tie another half inch as I introduced myself.

"This heat's driving me crazy. I'm absolutely on fire." She pulled one of the ice cubes out of her glass and ran it across her décolletage.

It was hard to ignore the ice melting on her chest, but I powered through. "Maurice Escargot was my partner."

"Was?"

"Was. You see him tonight?"

She took another drink. "He should be here any time."

I walked over and poured myself a drink. Made it neat.

"He will be here soon, right?"

I gulped down my whiskey. She slumped down into Escargot's only chair.

"Did he buy the farm?" she asked.

I nodded.

"What happened?" Her voice shook, but her hand remained steadily grasping the glass.

The answer flashed in my mind, still in black and white. The puddle under the desk looked like ink instead of the three quarts of blood it was. His head looked plastic, like an oversized baby doll head. Like a larger version of the six doll heads lined up next to it, three on the right, three on the left. The large head in the middle and the six toy heads each had one eye open and one closed.

I poured myself another drink.

"I found him at his desk." Or at least most of him.

"He do it to himself?"

"Doubtful."

"You sure?"

"His head was sliced clean off."

She took a drink. After she swallowed, she laughed. A low chuckle that built into a gut-busting laugh.

"If anyone could cut off their own head, it would be Maurice. He is such a klutz."

"Was."

She stopped laughing. "Was."

"Any idea who had it in for him?"

"Everyone. No one."

I nodded. No one liked the sonofa-bitch, but he was more of a threat to himself than anything. I did most of the heavy lifting at the firm. If anyone should be sitting headless at their desk with a fifth of Seagram's on the desk and a fifth of their own blood under their seat, it should be me.

I nervously rubbed my neck. "Any idea what he was working on?"

"Shouldn't you know that? You are his partner."

"Was."

"Was."

I heard stomping in the hall. The flatfoots were on their way.

I put my glass on the counter, my hat on my head, and headed toward the rear window. I opened it and swung my right foot over the sill and onto the fire escape. As I ducked my head under the top of the window frame, I saw it on the corner of the ledge. A plastic baby doll head. With one eye closed.

"You know about that?"

"Looks like a baby doll head."

I didn't have time to ask follow-up questions of Madame Obvious. I slipped the winking head into my pocket and hurried my exit down the fire escape.

After rushing down five flights, I jumped down into the alley next to an empty black and white.

"Attention all cars." The wireless in the front seat was turned up to full volume. "Be on the lookout for one cut-rate private dick calling himself Bass Levin. Wanted for questioning in the murder of his partner. Considered insane and dangerous. Use of excessive force is highly encouraged."

I pulled my fedora lower over my eyes and stomped off down the street. I was more angered about the dispatcher pronouncing my name Bahss, like the fish, rather than Base, like the jazz instrument, than the fact they wanted to stitch me up for the murder.

I didn't kill Maurice Escargot. But someone did. They sliced his head clean off. And not just his.

I peeked around the corner of the building, looking up and down the main drag. It was still deserted. I walked under the streetlamp and pulled the severed baby doll head from my pocket. It wasn't sliced clean like Escargot's head had been. It was ripped off. As I turned it in my fingers, I felt something. A nick maybe? I gave it a closer look. It wasn't a nick. It was a tooth mark.

What kind of sick sonofabitch bites the heads off baby dolls?

I slunk back into the shadows as I did a mental inventory of our caseload.

We weren't working on anything other than a couple of divorces that I thus far had found bupkis on. Escargot had been busting my chops about me not getting him the money shot. He kept prints of the surveillance shots "for the records" and was looking forward to adding nudies of Mrs. Dali to his collection. I had been looking forward to it myself, but it was even too hot for Mrs. Dali to fuck the milkman.

I decided to take another look at my only lead. I paused under the light at the back door of the butcher shop and gave the baby doll head another once over. I pulled open the closed eye. Or the eyelid covering what should have been an eye. The plastic eyeball had been removed. There was a slip of paper crammed into the empty socket. I reached in my pocket, grabbed my toothpick, and pried it out.

Three words were scrawled on the scrap of paper: <u>With Love, Jesus</u>.

Jesus? Had Escargot found religion? Unlikely. Was he batting for both teams? That was even more gobbledygook.

Then who was Jesus, and why was he sending love via the eye socket of a bitten-off baby doll head?

I pondered the question as I walked along the alley sweating through Escargot's borrowed shirt.

My God, it's hot tonight!

The summer night was now ragging me so hard I was blithering nonsense.

Doot Doot Dah, Dah Dah Dah Dah Dah Dum.

I stopped and listened. The dogs were still barking in the distance. The cats were still screaming. The road rats were still hiding, but there was a new noise. A catchy rhythm.

Doot Doot Dah, Dah Dah Dah Dah Dah Dum.

I looked around, trying to find the source. As I examined the backsides of the two-story shops lining the narrow lane, I suddenly realized where I was. All the random turns and attempts to stay hidden in the shadows had taken me back to the same place I started: the alleyway behind the office.

Doot Doot Dah, Dah Dah Dah Dah Dah Dum.

The sound came out of the back door of Paul's Boutique, the store beneath our office.

I had never once stepped inside the bodega in the five years we had the office.

That was about to change.

I tried the knob. It turned freely in my hand.

Doot Doot Dah, Dah Dah Dah Dah Dah Dum. The noise was getting louder.

I walked in the back door. It shut behind me, eliminating all but a faint light from the alleyway lamp coming through the window above the door frame. It was enough illumination to see shadows of boxes and mop buckets lining the hallway. After successfully navigating the hallway maze, I went around a corner and into the store.

The door to the hallway slammed behind me.

It was even darker in the store. I found the aisle between the shelves and followed it toward the front counter.

As I approached the front counter, my eyes had adjusted to the dark enough to make out the labels of some of the canned goods on the shelves. Confident with my newfound ability to see, I picked up the pace. If the bodega was worth its salt, it'd have cigarettes on the wall behind the counter. I could use a new pack if it ever got cool enough to start smoking again.

There weren't any cigarettes behind the front counter.

Whatever had been behind the register had been removed, and the racks had been yanked out of the wall. Seven headless baby dolls were stuck to the wall, each impaled by a dagger, next to the holes where the rack braces had been.

As I crept closer, I could see they had their limbs ripped from their bodies. Two of the dolls with cloth bodies had stuffing falling out of the four cor-ners where the appendages used to be. One of the all-plastic ones had its four limbs crammed in the neck cavity.

The plastic bodies had dark lines flowing from the chest wound. Dried blood? I couldn't be sure. There wasn't enough light in the room to see any-thing but the outlines of the victims. Yet I knew it was dried blood.

Whose blood? That I didn't want to know.

A row of baby dolls was lying on the counter, a solid dozen of them. Some had arms. Some had legs. Some had neither. Some had heads with one eye gouged out. Some had blood oozing from their remaining eye.

Whose blood? I still didn't want to know.

I began to walk backward, retracing my steps to get out from behind the counter.

"Hot tonight, ain't it?"

The voice came from right behind me.

I turned to find a figure standing directly in my escape path. A figure brandishing a machete.

"Jesus?" I tried to sound calmer than I was.

"It's pronounced Hay-Soos. Why can't anyone get that right, Bass Levin?" He smiled after pronouncing my name like the fish.

"Apologies."

"Bygones. I go by a different name now anyway."

"Which is?"

He ran his finger around the outline of one of the headless baby dolls on the wall. "I hear you killed your partner."

"It's a bum rap. We both know that."

He began tapping the sword on the metal counter.

Doot Doot Dah, Dah Dah Dah Dah Dah Dum.

"Quite the riff, isn't it? I hear it all the time. In here." He tapped his forehead with the sword, using the same cadence. "All the time."

"This heat is enough to make us all a little crazy."

He drove the sword into the wall, re-stabbing one of the dolls. "I made the heat!"

I looked around, trying to see where else swords may be hidden. I wished I had thought to take Escargot's snub-nose off the desk earlier. One should always bring a gun to a knife fight. Instead, I brought a severed baby doll head. I did not like those odds.

"You've done a bang-up job with the heat. Who should I be congratulating if you aren't Jesus anymore?"

He grabbed another sword from under the counter behind him.

"I've been toying with the name Lucy. Lucy Fur." He swirled the sword in the air. "But as your partner pointed out, that is a broad's name."

"Was."

"Was?"

"It was a broad's name. Now it is yours."

He held the sword up to my neck. "I like the cut of your jib, Bass."

"Thank you." I could feel the coolness of the blade lightly touching me. I swallowed, relishing the action while it was still possible. "Thank you, Lucy."

He lowered the sword.

"I've soured on Lucy. There's no need to be clever or coy. Just call me the Devil's Demon."

Even just having the bullets would have helped. I could have heated them with my lighter, igniting the powder to create a distraction. I might have lost an eye, but I was set to lose that and the rest of my head without them.

"Is that why you lobbed off his head? Because he wouldn't call you Lucy or the Devil's Demon?"

"No!"

He picked up a doll torso off the counter and skewered it to the wall with his sword.

"Then why?"

He grabbed another sword from under the counter and began tapping it on the ceiling.

Doot Doot Dah, Dah Dah Dah Dah Dah Dum. Doot Doot Dah, Dah Dah Dah Dah Dah Dum.

"He did it! He wrote that fucking song!"

The nutjob formerly known as Jesus, who was called Lucy for a hot second before rebranding himself as the Devil's Demon, paused. As he did, I could hear footfalls above in our office. It was the coppers walking the crime scene above our heads.

"Doot Doot Dah, Dah Dah Dah Dah Dah Dum. All the time. It's all I could hear. Even after I went home at night, I could still hear the song in my head. Doot Doot Dah, Dah Dah Dah Dah Dah

Dum. Doot Doot Dah, Dah Dah Dah Dah Dah Dum."

It was starting to make sense, or at least as much sense as the rantings of a man who claims to have made the heat could make. Escargot was a habitual pacer. It was how he thought. He walked back and forth through the office in the same pattern over and over. The pattern of the riff.

<u>Doot Doot Dah, Dah Dah Dah Dah Dah Dum</u>.

If he'd only been a lazy sonofabitch who sat on his fat ass all day instead of a skinny prick who walked off his nervous energy, he'd still have a head.

"I just wanted to know the rest of the song. But he said he didn't write it. You do not lie to the Devil's Demon. There are consequences when you lie to the Devil's Demon."

He took a big swing with the sword. As he swung it back to the left, he suddenly stopped and brought the weapon back to the front. Back pointing directly at me.

"Was it you? Were you the one who wrote the song?"

I gulped, again appreciating that my Adam's apple was still present and correct. But probably only for a minute longer.

There was no way to answer that question and remain headed.

My only play was to get behind him, where he seemed to be hiding his arsenal, and grab a sword. Even if I got there and armed myself without him slashing me, I would have to go head-to-head with a veteran murderer who, given the rogue's gallery of baby doll carnage on the wall, was pretty handy with a sword. And who may or may not be the spawn of Satan.

It was too hot for a sword fight.

"I didn't write the song."

I closed my eyes and readied for impact.

My life flashed before me, the visions again in black and white. Images of broads, bars, and butts—cigarette butts. I jumped to the office, watching Maurice Escargot pour himself one last whiskey moments before losing his head.

I heard the woosh of a blade cutting through the air but didn't feel a slice through my neck. After a moment, I realized I was still alive. I tentatively opened my eyes, one at a time.

Before me stood the headless body of Lucy Fur. His head was on the ground at his feet. As I tried to make sense of the scene, his body crumpled to the floor. Blood spilled from the hole between his shoulders, puddling around his head. In the dim lighting of the room, it all seemed to be happening in black and white. It was better that way. It was too gruesome for Technicolor.

Behind his head was a pair of snakeskin shoes. My eyes scanned the long legs attached to the shoes. It was Angel standing behind him, holding a bloody sword.

Angel was definitely one tough broad.

I walked over and took the sword from her. She pulled out a pack of smokes and put one in her mouth.

"I loved that goofy sonofabitch."

I nodded and lit her cigarette. She took a long drag off it.

I gave her my hand as she stepped out of the pool of blood. She took off her shoes and handed them to me. I put them in my left hand, placed my right around her waist and led her to the back door. We silently walked into the alleyway.

It was too hot to ask questions.

It was too hot to clean up a crime scene.

It was too hot in this town for the two of us.

I reached into my pocket and found the baby doll head from Escargot's apartment. I tossed it down the sewer grate as we headed into the distance.

Author Inspiration

There is such a strong sense of place and time created by the <u>Lace and Whiskey</u> album. I enjoyed slipping into that black-and-white world and finding the horror noir within. This story isn't as graphic or edgy as others within this collection but holds true to both the spirit of the genre and the album, especially this story's titular song. It felt too obvious to write a story from the point of view of Maurice Escargot, the "hero" of the album, so instead I chopped off his head.

"Desperado"
by Jason R Frei

The sun hovered directly overhead when he rode into the small town of Tell's Ford on his pale Appaloosa. The wide, flat brim of his hat rode low, obscuring his face in its shadow. His long, black hair trailed behind him like a cape. Dirt and grime from the road etched itself into the cracks of his black leather jacket. White lace peeked out from the jacket and bone-white ruffles poked out from the sleeves.

He hitched his horse to the post in front of the saloon and made his way inside, his spurs jangling on the wooden floorboards. The room grew silent as he ambled to the bar. He lifted his head, and the barkeep staggered back, crossing himself.

"El Desperado," whispered a Mexican at the end of the bar.

The face that glanced out from under the hat was painted up like a demented clown. Heavy, black paint circled his hazel eyes. A single thin line slashed each eye from mid-forehead down to the cheekbone. His mouth was carved in a cruel slash over a lined and worn face.

He was known simply as Desperado. No one knew his true name or where he came from, but they knew his function, his purpose. He was a cold-blooded killer. For twenty dollars, he would kill any man, woman, or child. The notches on his gun belt held the stories of twenty-three victims.

"Whiskey," he growled to the barkeep.

The barkeep's hands shook as he poured most of the whiskey onto the bar. Desperado grabbed the bottle from him, sending the man reeling backward. The killer upended the bottle and took a long slug, cleaning the dust from his throat. When he slammed the bottle down, it was empty. He threw a coin on the bar and turned to the crowd.

"I'm looking for Lady Chen."

A few whispers rippled through the group, but not a single man looked him in the eye. He pushed off the bar and walked slowly around the room.

"You already know who I am, and now you know why I'm here."

He rolled a gold coin across his knuckles as he walked. The light played off its surface, dancing between the ridged edge and the silver of the rings on his fingers. A few of the men licked their lips, itching to test the coin between their teeth, see if it was real gold or not. He stopped in front of a young man—a boy really, barely old enough to grow peach fuzz on his cheeks. He set the coin down in front of him, spun a chair around and sat down with his arms across the back of it.

He leaned in close to the boy. "All you have to do is point, and it's yours."

The boy looked into the face of the hired killer, and a shudder went down his spine. The scent of lavender wafted across the boy's nostrils. He gulped and slid a solitary finger out, pointing north. Desperado grinned, causing a dandy of a man at the next table to faint. He clapped the back of the boy's hand, stood, and left the saloon.

Desperado looked up at the sign on the building. It read "The Painted Cat" in multi-colored letters. A crude, painted Siamese cat with red lipstick and blue eye shadow lounged across the letters.

The brothel was the second largest building in town, only shorter than the saloon by a few feet. At this time of day, none of the ladies sat on the porch, enticing customers inside. The brothel was a night business, which meant this was the perfect time for him to conduct his.

He walked through the front door and was assaulted by an overwhelm-ing deluge of smells—smoke from a thousand cigars and cigarettes and pipes, perfumes of a myriad of scents ranging from floral to musk, the primal stench of sex and sweat and human debauchery. Underlying it all was another familiar scent. The scent of death.

He stood for a moment, clearing his head of the olfactory overload. The bordello was quiet. Most of the girls still slept in their rooms. A few lazed about on couches, their heads filled with thoughts of sleep or clouded with the smoke of hashish and opium. Two mostly-nude women sat at a table spooning large amounts of runny eggs into each other's mouths and giggling.

Bacon fried, hissing and spitting, on an untended iron stove top in the corner.

A woman stumbled past, her dress longer than her legs. He caught her by the arm before she could fall.

"Lady Chen?" he inquired.

She nodded to a set of stairs in the corner wall. Her eyes were almost closed. He walked her to the nearest chair, where she plopped down and promptly started snoring. He gently brushed her hair from her face and leaned her head against a pillow. She reminded him of a girl from a long time ago, back before he was this man.

At the top of the stairs, two big Indians—Cherokee from the look of them—

straight and silent like wooden cigar store statues, guarded a door. Corridors led off to the sides. He presumed the girls' rooms were down there.

He leaned his back against the wall and crossed his arms. "I'm here to see Lady Chen."

The Indian closest to him smiled but said nothing.

"So, do I just knock, or are you going to get the door for me?"

The smiling Indian reached out a beefy hand to grab the hitman's shirt. Within seconds, the Cherokee was on his knees on the floor, his arm straight out behind him and the joints in his wrist, elbow, and shoulder straining to stay in their sockets. Desperado let his arm go and in one fluid motion, shoved the aggressor down the stairs with a boot to the backside.

The other Indian pulled out a hatchet and swung at the killer. Desperado dodged to the side and drove his shoulder into the larger man's midsection. He planted his feet and thrust hard, driving the big Indian through the door. Momentum and force combined to shatter the door into small splinters that flew through the room like shrapnel.

The Cherokee was up in an instant and heaved his hatchet at his enemy. The smaller man plucked it out of the air as if grabbing an errant feather in the breeze. His lip curled up to one side in a mocking sneer.

"Enough!" The word echoed through the room like the sudden clap of thunder.

Desperado threw the hatchet, sticking it in the floor in front of the Cherokee's feet. He then turned toward the woman who had called out. She sat at a table with two others. To her right was Dos Santos, a big Mexican with a chest tattoo. His long, black- and gray-streaked hair hung in his face. Rumor had it the gunfighter was dead, but rumors abounded out here in the West.

To her left sat Madison, a skinny, ginger gringo with a broom handle mustache. Desperado had heard the name in hushed whispers but never had the opportunity to meet him.

"To what do I owe this pleasure?" asked Lady Chen. She was a middle-aged Chinese woman who wore a simple red silk kimono. A long cigarette dangled from her fingers, fingers that ended in sharp lacquered nails.

He eyed her suspiciously. "I've come to collect on your bounty."

She laughed, a high musical titter that rang through the room. He felt a presence behind him and turned as the second Cherokee filled the doorway, his arms across his chest, the smile replaced with a scowl.

"Is that so?" Lady Chen took a drag from her cigarette and blew it out, quick and hard. The smoke formed an arrow that darted across the room and dissipated against Desperado's chest. The smoke was pungent—bitter and acrid.

He rolled his shoulders and cracked his knuckles. Desperado eyed the four other men in the room then fixed Lady Chen with a glower.

"I'll be back at sunset to collect."

He spun around quickly, catching the Cherokee at the door by surprise and twisted him back into the room like a waltz partner. He tipped his hat and nonchalantly spur-jangled down the stairs.

439

Shortly before dusk, Desperado stepped out of the bar. The sheriff stood at the bottom of the stairs, holding the reins to the Appaloosa.

"Evening, sheriff."

The sheriff was a skinny feller. His clothes hung loose on his lanky frame. His hat was too big for his head, and he looked like he might step out of his boots at any minute. In all, he looked like a child playing dress-up.

"We don't want no trouble in this here town, sir. Think it would be best for all of us if you just hitched up in this saddle and rode off into the night."

"Can't do that, son. I got a job to do, and ain't no one getting in my way."

The sheriff put his free hand on the butt of his pistol.

Desperado smiled his crooked smile. "I like your gumption, sheriff, but we both know how that would end."

The killer ambled down the steps and removed the reins from the sheriff's shaking hand. He produced a gold coin from out of the air, walked it across his knuckles, and tossed it to the lawman.

"This is for any of the material damages that might occur. Keep everyone inside the saloon, and don't come out until morning. I promise, you and your townsfolk will be safe."

Desperado didn't wait for an answer. He turned and walked down the street with his horse in tow.

He was a few yards from the brothel when the horse let out a whinny and reared up on its hind legs. Its eyes were round and showed too much white. He tried to calm the horse, but it was obviously spooked. A sound from behind caused him to drop the reins and spin into a crouch. The horse reared again, its front hooves flashing out over Desperado's head. A large, furry bulk changed direction at the last moment and hurtled past the assassin.

Desperado forward-rolled and came back up on his feet with a Bowie knife in hand. The full moon loomed large over the town, and its light reflected off the wicked blade. The hirsute mass, a werewolf, stood, towering almost eight feet tall. It lumbered toward its target, stopping short several feet from the man.

Drool slavered from its massive jaws. Fierce amber eyes looked out from its lupine head. Sharp, black talons extended from its elongated fingers. Reddish-brown hair covered its body.

Desperado crossed an arm in front of his chest and bowed, the brim of his hat almost touching the ground. "Good evening, Mister Madison. It's a pleasure to make your acquaintance."

The wolf-man snorted, his lips curled back from his pointed teeth. He made his own mock bow in return.

Desperado tightened his grip on the knife. "You can walk away now and leave with your skin intact. I'm only here for the woman."

A low chortle came from the wolf's throat. He bent forward, lowering his head and extending his arms out to his sides. In less than a blink, his powerful legs bunched, and he leaped at his prey.

Desperado barely dodged the oncoming attack. He slid his knife deftly across Madison's ribs. The wolf howled in pain and clutched at his side.

"Silver," said the gunslinger, brandishing the blade. "Stings like a bitch, don't it?"

The werewolf roared in anger and charged. Desperado attempted to side-step the attack, but the beast saw the move, pivoted, and thrust out a mighty claw. The swipe caught the clown-faced cowboy across the chest. Four lacerations appeared through silk and leather and flesh. Blood stained the front of his shirt.

Anger flashed in the assassin's eyes. "That was my last clean shirt."

He launched himself at the beast, connecting a left hook to the wolf's chin. Madison staggered back, welts raised where the silver rings had touched him. Desperado fought furiously, landing punch after punch, slicing through fur and flesh with the Bowie knife.

The man's attacks were quick and relentless. Madison dodged and weaved with no time to make a counterstrike. Blood matted the werewolf's fur, and his strength ebbed and faltered.

The wolf-man was pushed against the front wall of the brothel. He made one last ditch effort by pushing off and swinging his powerful arms. Desperado ducked as the claws whistled over his head. He sprung and drove the blade into the werewolf's throat, angled up under the jaw. Hot blood gushed over the blade and his hand. Madison made a pitiful mewling sound, then his eyes rolled back in his head, and he dropped to the ground.

The assassin watched as the beast shriveled and shrank in on itself until only the man was left. He pulled out the knife and wiped the blood onto his pants. He stood over the corpse with his eyes closed and his head bowed. After a moment, he bent and crossed Madison's arms over his chest. He placed two silver coins over the dead man's eyes.

"May you find the peace you deserve in the afterlife."

Inside the brothel, the parlor was dark and quiet, not like a brothel should be at night. Desperado stood in the gloom, allowing his eyes to adjust. He caught the scent of tobacco and musk, and turned quickly, catching a glancing blow from a meaty fist. The Cherokee who'd smiled at him earlier pivoted and swung again. Desperado barely dodged the punch before another fist hit him from behind. The second Cherokee grunted his satisfaction.

The cowboy slid the knife from its sheath and positioned himself so his attackers were in front of him. The two Indians looked at each other and nodded.

One of them circled to his left. Desperado tracked him and stepped back to give more room. Before he could react, the other Cherokee opened his fist and blew a fine powder into the painted face. The assassin's eyes burned, and snot flowed freely from his nose. Two bright splashes of light erupted in the blurry darkness.

Desperado slid backward across the room until he hit a wall. He blinked rapidly to clear his eyes.

The Cherokees no longer stood in the room. Instead, two old, withered, corvid-headed creatures had replaced them. Skin the color of

red clay dirt stretched over scraw-
ny muscle and sinew. Arms so long
they almost reached the floor were
tipped with thin, black claws. Scrag-
gly, black-feathered wings jutted from
their knobby-boned backs. Eyes like
flint peered from the raven skulls that
made up their heads. Each creature
emitted a fiery light from their bodies.

"Raven Mockers," said Desperado.
His voice held a hushed tone of awe.

At the same time, both Raven Mockers opened their beaks and let out a
raucous, shrill caw, then they attacked.

Although the creatures appeared
old and decrepit, they had a cunning
and agility that made them dangerous.
They took turns running in, feinting

and attacking, always keeping Desperado on his toes, always looking for a
chink in his armor. He slashed out with
his knife, doing little damage, although
the air was soon thick and choked with
black feathers. He yearned to pull his
pistols and end the fight but knew that
he would need them for Lady Chen
and whatever tricks she had up her
kimono sleeve.

The killer stumbled as he took an
errant swing, and the Raven Mockers
took this as their chance at victory. All
they managed to do was get in each
other's way. Their wings smacked
against each other and interlocked,
pinning them together.

"If I don't do something now, I may never get to the woman," mumbled Desperado.

In a flash, his ivory-handled Peacemaker leapt from its holster to his hand and a deafening report filled the parlor. His aim was true as always, and the bullet flew through both hearts that were in perfect alignment. Fragments of bone and muscle blew out behind them, making a splattered mess of the upholstered couches and chairs.

The weary man plucked the longest feather from each Raven Mocker. "These will make a nice addition to my hat band."

He slung his gun back into its holster, sheathed his knife, and headed up the stairs. He noticed again how quiet it was. His tread on the stairs was the only sound.

The door at the top of the stairs was still missing from the afternoon ruckus. One hinge sat crooked in the frame. Moonlight slanted through a window, bathing the room in a silver glow. A single chair sat in the middle of the room, and in the chair sat Dos Santos. His head was bowed, his greasy, black-and-gray hair hanging over his face.

"I'm going to give you the same deal I offered Madison. Walk away and no harm will come to you."

Dos Santos said nothing, didn't even move a muscle. Desperado leaned in with his head cocked to the side, listening. No sound came from the seated man. The gunslinger watched the man intently and took a step back when he realized the man was not breathing. There was neither rise nor fall of the chest, no imperceptible shake of the shoulders that a breathing man would have.

Desperado took a few steps into the room. He was within arm's reach when Dos Santos lifted his head and stared at the intruder. The moon's radiance illuminated the face. His eyes were gray, the color of dull iron. Black lines, like spider webs, stretched out across the man's face. Part of his cheek was missing, as if chewed through. His teeth, rotten and yellow, peeked out from the fleshy window.

The gunslinger recoiled at the sight and jumped back. Dos Santos stood. His thin leather vest flapped open. His entire front torso was tattooed with an image of the Virgin Mary facing and holding hands with her Mexican counterpart, Our Lady of Guadalupe. Two large bullet holes cratered in his chest where the ladies held hands. The assassin froze momentarily, just long enough for the large Mexican to grab him by the jacket in an iron grip.

Dos Santos lifted his quarry like he was an empty sack. Desperado rained ineffective blows down on the Mexican as his feet swung free of the floor. The dead man pivoted and threw the living one through the air. He hit the wall and crumpled to the floor.

Before he could pull in a breath, Dos Santos was on him again. He was flung around the room time and time again like a rag doll. While the dead man needed no breath for his exertions, the living man's came in great ragged gasps. Blood trickled from mouth and nose, landing on his already-ruined shirt.

Before he could be hurled again, Desperado pushed off the wall and rolled under the reaching hands of the Mexican. He sprinted to the other side of the room, near the exit, spun with his gun in his hand and pulled off four shots in a row. Each bullet thudded solidly into Dos Santos, who jerked back with every hit until his back was against the wall.

The smoking gun held one last bullet. The gunslinger squared off his stance, held the gun in both hands, aimed at his enemy's head and pulled the trigger. Dos Santos' head burst like an overripe melon in the sun and left a wet splash on the wall behind him. The body slumped and moved no more.

Desperado heard a soft sound behind him and turned, his gun poised.

"Rust."

The word whispered through the room from the lips of Lady Chen, who stood just outside the door. The gun in his hand turned red and pitted. The metal flaked and disintegrated into a pile on the floor. Six brass shell casings lay in a pile of rusty dust. Only the ivory-handled grip remained in his hand.

Lady Chen balled her hand into a fist and squeezed. Desperado dropped to one knee, clutching his chest. He clenched his teeth to lock in a scream.

The Chinese witch laughed. She entered the room and circled, slowly, warily, around the man.

"You had me worried for a moment," she said.

Her voice buzzed in his head, as if a thousand flies had hatched and were feasting on his brain. A moan escaped through his clamped lips. Sweat dripped down his face, and droplets splashed the floor in front of him. His eyes blurred, and his senses felt like day-old oatmeal.

Lady Chen pulled up a chair and sat in front of the wheezing man. She took off his hat and grabbed his hair, pulling his head back to face her.

"You've failed." There was no meanness, no harshness in her words, just brutal honesty. "Who sent you?"

Drool mixed with blood dripped from Desperado's mouth. The paint around his eyes was streaked and blurred. He tried to smile, but there was too much pain to be more than a grimace. He grunted a few unintelligible syllables.

Lady Chen shook his head. "I won't ask again. Who sent you?"

His chest and shoulders shook as laughter bubbled up from his core. Even through all the pain, he defied the woman. She sighed then squeezed her fist so hard her knuckles cracked.

The would-be assassin cried out in anguish and pitched forward. She slammed her fist into her other hand. A loud report echoed through the room, like a gunshot. Desperado's cry was cut short. His body lay still.

Lady Chen knelt before the fallen man and whispered in his ear. "Not even the Devil himself can kill me."

She made to stand when Desperado flipped over and grabbed her by the throat in an iron-grip.

"That's why he sent me," he whispered.

He grabbed her hair and pulled her head to the side. With an inhuman growl, he plunged his teeth into her neck and bit down. The salty tang of blood squirted into his mouth and spilled down his chin. Lady Chen struggled briefly then closed her eyes and went limp.

The sheriff looked out the window for the hundredth time. The sky was just starting to soften in the east, a rosy glow spreading into the sky. Snores and sounds of fitful sleeping filled the saloon. Other than the sheriff and the young man from the day before, all other patrons were asleep.

A set of footsteps sounded on the saloon's porch as the sky continued to brighten. The sheriff pulled his gun and aimed it at the door. There was silence for only a few breaths, then the door opened slowly. Desperado limped in. His face was ruddy and swollen— full. His eyes glinted like diamond chips in a pit of coal. Blood smeared his face and mixed with the makeup, further enhancing his already demonic appearance.

"Is it done?" asked the sheriff.

The gunslinger eyed the man and nodded his head.

"So, you'll be moving on then?"

Another nod.

The sheriff holstered his pistol.

"Thank you for keeping my town safe," said the sheriff.

"I had a job to do. Your people were never in any danger. At least, not from me," said Desperado. "Not everything you heard about me is true. Most, but not everything."

He turned to the door when the boy spoke up.

"Which one got away?"

The gunslinger turned back. "What do you mean?"

The boy pointed at the fresh gouges on the killer's belt. "There's only four notches on your belt."

Desperado flashed his lopsided grin. "I reckon Dos Santos belongs on someone else's belt on account of him being dead before I shot him."

The sheriff nodded. "Where will you go now?"

Wearily, Desperado shrugged his shoulders. "Wherever I'm needed. There's always more souls to send back to hell."

He left the saloon and mounted his pale horse. With a wave, Death rode

out of Tell's Ford, on his way to har-
vest more lost souls.

Author Inspiration

I've been an Alice Cooper fan since I was a kid. I picked "Desperado" because it reminded me of Saturdays with my dad. We used to watch TV together all day—old westerns, <u>The Twilight Zone</u>, <u>The Outer Limits</u>, the Three Stooges, and B-rated horror movies like <u>Attack of the 50 Foot Woman</u>. This story is those Saturdays with my dad.

"Inside Me"

by Shannon Lawrence

Her lips are sweetly spiced with cinnamon and sugar from churros shared amidst the jangling violence of a carnival. They're soft, yet hungry, against mine. I'd kiss her all night if she'd let me.

When she pulls away, it takes me a moment to open my eyes. My lips feel bruised and full from the rush of blood to them. She's smiling, lips and cheeks all curves, eyes half-closed. I ache with the need for more.

"Goodnight," she says. Her fingers trail down my arm, leaving behind a warm reminder of their passage. Cold swirls around me in the absence of her body heat and sensual energy. A ghost of her presence lilts over my skin.

I watch her leave, the sway of her hips mesmeric. My breath catches when she turns to look back at me one more time, and I raise a hand in an awkward wave. Her long hair glides like silk over her shoulders when she turns away again.

The short walk to my apartment passes in a blur of physical memory, my body a tyranny of pleasant sensations and yearnings that overwhelm my senses.

Then the tingling begins in my lips, gentle at first, but growing in urgency. They're warm as if I've eaten hot chilies. I run my fingers over them and find they are hot to the touch and pulsating. It takes me a minute to realize they're pulsing in time with my heartbeat.

At first, I smile. It reminds me of her, of where I was just an hour ago. As first dates go, this was the best I'd ever been on. A chance meeting at the library, numbers exchanged, a date set up. I hadn't expected her to answer when I called, nor did I think she'd accept my invitation. But she had. My very own dream girl, and she liked me back.

Conflicted, I type out a series of texts telling her what a great time I had, erasing each one after a moment of thought. Maybe it's too soon to contact her. I don't want to come across as needy or psychotic. Finally, I suck it up and send a text that says _Thinking of you. I had fun tonight._ There's nothing creepy about that.

The warmth in my lips intensifies, a raging fire. It feels as if my skin will slough off. I lick them, the cinnamon-sugar lingering. Racing to the kitchen, I open the fridge and shift items on the top shelf until I find the milk. My hands shake as I pour it into a glass. Some of it spills onto the counter, the floor, my shirt. Heedlessly,

I gulp the milk down. It pours down my chin, soaking my shirt even more.

The heat does not abate.

I open the freezer and pull an ice cube out of the bin, rubbing it over my lips. It melts rapidly without bringing any relief. I can barely feel the cold through the intensity of the heat. My lips throb with it.

Grabbing another ice cube, I make my way to the bathroom. Not sure what I expect, I study my mouth in the mirror. My lips are visibly swollen as if I'd been stung by a bee. They're bright red, the color expanding out- ward, creeping across my face, down my chin and up to my nose. Somehow, seeing that they look as bad as they feel makes the pain worse. Once more, I try to soothe them with the ice cube, now half-melted in my hand. It turns to liquid within seconds, a mist rises from my lips.

With dawning horror, I realize I can see them moving, squirming. This isn't just the pulsating I felt earlier. Something is under the skin. Inside my lips.

My phone buzzes, indicating a text. I ignore it.

When I press a finger to my lips, they writhe beneath it. There are small, worm-like movements. I put my face close to the mirror and squint to see better. There are green things moving under my skin, dim against the red of my lips. They seem to be multiplying and growing quickly. As I watch, my lips swell further, the surface undulating with the movement within.

My phone buzzes again. This time I take it out and press the text preview to bring it up. She's written me back: <u>The night's not over yet.</u>

I shove my phone into my back pocket once again and press my lips closed. Something has to make them feel better, to bring me some relief. It can't be what it looks like. There's absolutely no way this is happening.

The green things are roiling, pressing against my swollen flesh. They started out the thickness of thread, but they've now become the size of spaghetti. One breaks free of my lips, the green now vibrant against the paleness of the skin surrounding them. It wiggles and inches its way along, working itself down into my chin.

More worms break free, pressing into the flesh surrounding my lips. They look like veins. Only veins don't move like maggots.

Another buzz vibrates my phone. I don't want to see what she's said now.

Instead, I race back to the kitchen, digging through the drawers. I toss aside a wooden spoon, a slotted spoon, mixer blades. I'm not sure what I'm looking for until I see the zester lying in the bottom of the drawer, buried beneath the rest of my cooking utensils. I grab that and a pair of tongs and return to the bathroom mirror.

The buzz comes again. I set the zester and tongs on the edge of the sink and pull out my phone to read the newest texts.

I'm inside you.

Can you feel me?

This time I toss my phone into the tub and return my full attention to my lips. It's not just them anymore. The worms have spread out, seeping like an infection into the rest of my face and down my neck. I can feel them working their way through my flesh. It's not entirely unpleasant. The burning discomfort has eased some, becoming more bearable. For the most part, their movement itches, even tickles. Mostly, it just feels foreign.

My phone vibrates against the porcelain of my old clawfoot tub, loud and echoing within the constraints of the space. It irritates me as the buzzing of a fly might.

The worms have grown more and multiplied. They are now the thickness of unstretched yarn. My face writhes with them now, one approaching my eye. I can't let this continue.

The itch has deepened, competing with the burning sensation. I find myself clawing at my skin without meaning to, leaving furrows that quickly fill with blood. It drips down my face, a crimson serpent. My skin looks like a disturbing road map of green and red lines. There's an intense pressure in my lips, which have become distended like burgeoning egg sacs, ready to burst. My teeth ache, and I realize I've been clenching my jaw.

The worm reaches the flesh of my lower eyelid and disappears, plunging out of sight as if it has gone deeper beneath the surface. Soon, I can't feel that one anymore.

Another one reaches my Adam's apple, and the rough sensation causes me to cough. A crack appears in my top lip. It's not meant to stretch this much. The worms still in response but start back up again almost right away.

They're now as big around as a phone charging cable. Pain has replaced the itching and burning, pure and sharp. I now know what a tree must feel as creatures burrow inside it, creating tunnels and laying eggs, slowly but surely overtaking its entrails. Every movement feels as if something is forcing its way through my face, digging away at my skin, rending the nerves. Another crack appears in my upper lip, followed by the first in my lower lip. My lips have ripened, preparing to give birth to the monstrous worms within.

Something presses at the back of my eye. There's an intense pressure, ceaseless, persistent.

Then it is through. It feels like an eyelash in my eye. It's a dull pain at first, but it sharpens and shifts. I can't stop blinking, tears forming only to spill from my eyes and run down my cheeks. The tears create clean swaths through the blood.

Leaning even closer to the mirror, I stare until the worm in my eye becomes visible. As the pain increases, I cannot keep my eyelids open. They shut against the pain. During the brief moments I'm able to open that eye, I realize I can see the shadow of the worm within. Not just in the mirror, but in my vision. It has grown once more, at least the thickness of a maggot, and it is tunneling through the viscous liquids of my eye.

Below, the worms have spread out, burrowing their way across my chest. I tear my shirt open, popping off a button. They're in my left breast, competing with the visible veins there. One works its way toward my areola. My skin feels like boiling water looks, a constant roiling beneath the surface. Sensations blur together, and I can no longer tell what burns, what hurts, and what itches. My lips are the worst of it, a confusion of agony and irritation.

My phone rings now, the music sounding canned as it rises from inside the tub. I ignore it, but it plays again and again until I can't take it anymore. I tear my eyes from the mirror and cross to the tub, retrieving the still intact phone. Not even a crack from having been thrown. I turn off the ringer and take the phone with me, setting it on the sink.

As the worm reaches my nipple, a strange burst of pleasure hits me, quickly overtaken by pain as the worm violates the nerve it just caressed.

The eye-worm is still in my vision, and it becomes hard to see with the shadow filling the space.

Picking up the zester, I steel myself for what's to come. The pressure in my lips has become unbearable. The first pass with the zester is tentative.

My nerves scream with the pain of it, and blood beads like crimson pearls on my lips before running down from them. Between the zester and the worms, the zester is the least of my pain. The second time is easier, sharp metal biting into my flesh, tearing at the nerves at the surface of my lips. A worm pokes from the mangled flesh left behind, and I seize the tongs, try to grab it. They're too unwieldy. Instead of the worm, I grab my lip, pinching it.

Dropping the tongs, I open the medicine cabinet and search for twee-zers, tossing medicine bottles, tooth-paste, a razor, my toothbrush, and more until my fingers find the comforting form of the tweezers. I close the medicine cabinet so I can use the mirror, and I zest my lips once more, this time also scraping across my chin. There's blood everywhere, my flesh maimed and looking vaguely of hamburger meat, but paler. More worms become visible, a much darker green than they'd appeared beneath the skin. With the tweezers, I grab one, pulling slowly, but firmly. It stretches, thins, and I fear it will break.

The worm writhes against my machinations, trying to free itself.

I pull harder.

Finally, the worm pops free, and I drop it into the sink, looking for another one. Ignoring the pain, I plunge the tweezers in after a worm just below the surface. Once more I stretch it out, pulling harder this time. It thins and resists my attempts. It has reached almost a foot in length, my hand far from my face. I feel the tug from within.

This time it snaps, sending one half of the worm slingshotting back into my flesh, where it quickly disappears. Like earthworms, these seem able to continue moving even after being severed. The half still clasped within the tweezers jerks and writhes. The blood that leaks from the severed end is blue.

I drop it in the sink and go in for another. They seem to know to avoid the surface now. They're going deeper.

My nipple screams with the pain of a worm eating its way through the sensitive nerves there, so I take up the zester once more and rake it across the raw nerves. The agony is exquisite. The worm there is the size of an earthworm, and I grasp it easily with my tweezers, pulling it slowly from my breast.

This time, I don't allow it to become too taut. It stretches, but I know not to pull to the breaking point this time. Even as I pull it on one side, the other part digs more deeply into my nipple, attempting to chew its way back inside me. I remember what I learned when fishing and both give and take, inching it out bit by bit, losing ground when necessary, only to regain it a moment later. The worm is plump and juicy, already well-fed from its time inside me. It glistens with my fluids.

When the worm finally breaks free, I am filled with a quick wash of relief and exhilaration, short-lived as it may be. Somehow the worms are propagating even more rapidly now, with what looks to be thousands of smaller worms spreading from the larger ones. The largest worm is the size of a wooden spoon handle. It's moving down my stomach. Every millimeter is misery, a shrieking chorus of nerves.

I try to use the zester over the large worm, but it isn't going deep enough. Each scrape fills with blood, blocking my view of the green creature inside me. I drop the zester and plunge the tips of the tweezers into my stom- ach above the center of the worm. It twitches inward, reacting to the stab. Then it quickly lengthens and keeps moving downward. I stab at it again, blind to the sensation of tiny stab wounds, so full of the feel of worms moving throughout my body now. The sense of movement within me is confusing, causing a sense of vertigo. Within and without, all is motion.

Wiggling the tweezers, I tear the skin further, allowing for easier egress. When blue blood mingles with the red of my own, I know I've reached the worm enough to grab it. I can feel it in the grasp of the tweezers, and I pull, careful not to sever its thick body with the intensity of my grasp.

I cough while struggling with the worm in my stomach, and tiny worms spray from my mouth. They splatter in the sink and against the mirror.

The worm pulls out in a long "U" shape, and I change my movements to try and pull one end out first. The tweezers are too sharp against the thicker worm, and they squeeze it, cutting through its body. I grasp the worm with my fingers, dropping the tweezers into the sink, desperate not to lose my grip. It feels thick and sinuous in my grasp, an ever-changing mass. It's so large that I wrap my entire hand around it and pull. It shouldn't be as strong as it is, but I'm losing against its ability to burrow with both sides of its body. No matter how much of it I get out, there's still more inside me.

The larger the worms get, the more the riotous sensations within me become pain, misery, agony.

A knock sounds at the door. It's late. No reason for anyone to be here. I'm too busy to check on it.

A strange, high whine is emitting from my throat. I'm scared, desperate, disgusted. I want these things out of me. I try to stop the sound, but it simply becomes more guttural. A scream waits at the back of my throat, a queue of terror.

The knock comes again. "It's me!" she calls through the absurdly thin door. "Let me in. I can help you."

I don't believe her. She did this to me. Why would she help?

One end of the worm breaks free from my skin, and I increase my grasp on it, pulling as hard as I can without breaking it. The end outside my body jerks crazily, thumping into my hand. It bites just below the knuckle of my index finger and starts burrowing into my hand.

I'm now fighting both ends of the worm in different places, but I'd rather have it in my hand than in my stomach. I ignore that end and continue yanking at the portion inside my stomach. There's a lot of bone in my hand for it to have to get around. That's what I tell myself.

She knocks again, and I walk toward the front door, still struggling with the worm. I grunt at the effort of fighting it, of the fine skill it takes not to tear it in half or let it go.

The worm in my eye has gotten so large that I can't see with that eye at all, and an incessant ache works its way backward into my skull. There's pressure like with my lips. It's going to burst at any moment.

My hand finds the lock, and I turn it before twisting the door handle. As the door opens, the worm pops from my stomach. I wrench its mouth from my hand and throw it on the floor, stepping on it and deriving a grim satisfaction from the sensation of it bursting beneath my shoe. Blue blood squelches from it, staining the floor. Still it squirms, but it doesn't concern me anymore.

Its brethren do.

I look up, my grin a rictus on my face. I must look feral.

My eye bursts, warm liquid running down my cheek. The worm inches across the bridge of my nose toward the other eye. I should be worried about it.

Yet there she is, as beautiful as she was earlier. She smiles at me and steps inside, shutting the door quietly behind her. I see now that beneath the lipstick her lips are blue. The fullness I'd so admired holds back a torrent of horror aching to spread. She touches my face and pulls me toward her, eyes intent on mine. I can't break free of her gaze or her grasp, and I lean in until her eyes blur enough that mine can close.

Despite the poison of her lips, I covet more.

Author Inspiration

Alice Cooper's song "Poison" takes forbidden love to a whole new level. A darker level. We often want things that harm us, whether a substance or a person. Two specific lines really stood out to me and inspired this story, where he says she has lips of venomous poison and that she was under his skin. Ultimately, our poison of choice draws us back in.

"Feed My Pugenstein"
by Bryan Stubbles

October 12, 1992

Dear Herk,
I'm starting this diary in memory of you. You were the kindest, most lovable, and most beloved pug that ever walked God's green Earth. Well, at least in Utah. You've been my friend since I was born, and now you left me for a better place. I hope there is a pug heaven where you can be the boss of all the pugs.

⚫ ⚫ ⚫

October 13, 1992

Dearest Herk,

We buried you today. It was a burial at sea. If only we'd had a 21 gun
salute! Well, actually, it was burial at
lake. Great Salt Lake. Dad drove me
out to the causeway. I remember before the lake flooded when I was six
and people could still visit Antelope
Island. I took you out to see the buf-
falo. Remember when one started to
cross the street and you barked at it
from inside the car? The poor thing
ran away! And he was like a thousand
pounds heavier than you. And he ran

away. Like a wuss. That was funny. Remember when we would run along the beach? That's all changed. The lake's gone down but the gate there is still chained up. You're unchained. You're free. You can do whatever you want now. Dad and I put you in a cardboard box and floated you off the shore. You drifted toward Antelope Island. I watched you disappear beneath the waves of Farmington Bay.

I hope you're happy. I'm not. Seventh grade sucks big time. Central Davis Junior High. I'm not kidding. They're so mean. Especially the girls. I call them the Social Clique Mafia. Jennifer P. attacked me today. I don't even know her. I said "Hi" to her and she said "Say 'Hi' again." So I did. She grabbed my ponytail and slammed my head into a locker. A teacher saw it, but he was too busy talking to some girls to do anything about it. People laughed. I wish I still had you.

October 14, 1992

Dear H,

I'm gonna call you "H." Herk is a cool name, but H is where it's at. Jennifer pretended she was gonna hit me. She didn't. I flinched. Other than that, school was tedious. In science we got to use a Bunsen burner. I'm a fan of the roaring blue flame. The Roaring

Blue Flames sound like a punk band. Bunsen burners and roaring blue flames can't fill the emptiness I feel without you.

October 15, 1992

Dear H,

Dad called the pound to see if they had any pugs. They didn't. They told him they almost never get pugs. Your kind is so popular, I guess. I begged him to go to the pound to check. Just in case. Maybe the worker forgot. Or didn't see all the dogs.

I really have the greatest dad. I don't know any other daughters whose dads would drive them to the pound.

The pound was awful! So many sad dogs. It's like they know they're gonna die. I know I'll die. No big deal, right? We just never know when or how. Death is the great equalizer.

There weren't any pugs for adoption at the pound, but I did find something worth my time. I need to make it real before I tell you about it.

October 16, 1992

Dear H,

I have such exciting news for you. My plan worked. See, the pound is in a town called Fruit Heights. I attached two baskets to my bike. I started around Main Street in Layton. I caught the 70 bus going south. I got off at Kaysville's Main Street and biked my way east toward the mountain. All of Davis County is hemmed in by majestically awesome mountains on the east and the Great Salt Lake on the west. You already know that. There wasn't any snow in the mountains. Sometimes there is. Sometimes it even snows on Halloween. You'd love that, wouldn't you?

Anyways, I made it to Fruit Heights. What a cute little town nestled in the foothills. My English teacher, Mrs. Mann, would probably call it "bucolic." Anyways, it's deceiving. That's where they kill all of Davis County's stray animals. You know how I know? It's connected to what I saw yesterday.

October 15, 1992 (again, duh)

Dear H,

So I'm going back in time to yesterday. Like a Beatles song. When I was with Dad, I saw a pile of white garbage bags behind the pound. I asked him if those were dead dogs. He said "Of course not. They just bury the dogs somewhere." Let's just say he's not a detail-oriented person.

He also told me to stop looking at the garbage. Well, I peeked one more time and guess what? I saw a pug face staring back at me! I was so excited, but I didn't tell anyone. Not even you. But now I can.

I hustled up there with my pink bike, flower basket, and the other basket I'd screwed on. It was dark by the time I got there. I brought an old Army flashlight. The pile of garbage bags was higher than before.

It was time to get dirty. I lugged through nasty garbage bags full of dead dogs. Mutts. Mongrels. Cute dogs. Chihuahuas. A Saint Bernard.

Aw, man! He was so freakin' heavy! A Shar Pei. Poor thing. All those dogs without homes. Without love. I found the pug. His face looked a little puffier than before. Then I saw something else. Another pug. Oh my gosh. And another. And another. Four dead pugs! I couldn't believe my luck!

I wrapped them up tight. I put one in the spud sack I had brought. Another was in the garbage bag in the basket. Somehow I got them all to balance oddly on my bike. It was all downhill from the pound.

I was craving a banana split. I cruised Kaysville's Main Street. My old standby, Dairy Queen, was open. I parked my bike outside and ran in.

Shelly was at the counter. I don't know why Shelly hates me so much. I swear I could see her roll her stupid little eyes even before I opened the door to come in. She turned to a co-worker in the back. I swear I heard her say:

"Look, it's the garbage lady," or something like that. She then turned to me all normal-like:

"Welcome to Dairy Queen. May I take your order?"

"I'm not the garbage lady," I told her.

"Are you mental?"

"No. I just want a hamburger."

"You came to a Dairy Queen for a hamburger?"

"It's on your ads," I said. I was too rattled by her attitude to order the banana split. Besides, making her use the grill was more rewarding than making her throw together a banana split.

"Anything else?"

I told her I wanted a water. She scoffed as she handed me a cup.

The burger came to $2.04 with tax. The water was free. I paid with coins I'd found around the house. Shelly had a nasty look on her face as she accepted the exact change from me.

I sat down at a window seat so I could keep an eye on my dogs. A worker brought out my burger. Usually they just put it on the tray on the counter. So this was kinda weird. I recognized the worker. Eve. Actually one of the nicer students.

"So we all have a bet on what's in your garbage bags," she said. "Mind if we have a look-see?"

"It's dead fuckin' pugs," I said. "But help yourself." I motioned to the bags. Eve stood there for what seemed like a minute staring out the window before Shelly yelled something at her. She ran back behind the counter.

The burger gave me enough calories to lug the pug corpses home. The water kept me hydrated.

There's a freezer in the garage behind my house. You know that, Herk. I stuck the garbage bags in the freezer.

Nobody will know they are there. Unless they want a popsicle. I'm so tired. Zzzz.

October 16, 1992

I did the most evil, vile, wicked thing I have done in my life. I almost borrowed a Van de Graaff generator from school today without asking. I'm sure you know what that is. It's a generator with a giant ball and a little ball. Mr. Reese conducts experiments with it. Well, more like demonstrations. We can see the sparks fly between the balls. I figured since our taxes paid for it, I could borrow it for the weekend.

I thought I was in the clear after the bell to go home rang today. I slipped into his classroom. I was going to steal it red-handed like a thief ... I mean borrow, but Mr. Reese caught me. I thought I was in trouble. You know how Mr. Reese is always trying to be alone with the girls? Well, that in-cludes me. Don't worry, nothing hap-pened. I just smiled a bunch, and he said I could borrow the Van de Graaff. What a nice teacher for a creepy guy.

The news. Man, what a mess. Clin-ton. Bush. Perot. I guess Perot is the most honest one. He'll probably lose. 519 people dead in an earthquake in Cairo. Willy Brandt is dead. Deion Sanders threw a tub of ice water on Tim McCarver. Scalpers are charging $750 dollars for Garth Brooks tickets. They can have them. Country music needs a savior, but it sure as hell ain't Garth.

To recover from that news, I put on my parents' record of Charley Pride. I played it while I experimented. What type of experiment? The one where I ran electricity through a pug's body in the garage. It wasn't you, Herk. But it could be. Well, the muscles moved. I made him wag his tail like you did. Remember that? You had such a cute tail. His isn't as cute. Kinda bony.

I can use electricity to make you whole again.

October 19, 1992

I had to give the Van de Graaff generator back to Mr. Reese today. He said I could get it any time I wanted.

Debbie bothered me at school today. Seems she heard I talked to Mr. Reese after class. She had a lot to say about it. Hurtful things. Awful things. It seems someone told her. But who?

October 20, 1992

I took my bike out to the lake to-day, looking for you. I didn't find you. I found some garbage. A 7-11 cup. A couple of plastic bags. There's always tomorrow.

October 21, 1992

Dear Herk,

I found you!!!!!! I found you, I found you, I found you!!!!!!!!!!!!!

You're a bit soggy. I left you in the garage to dry off. The other pugs will be happy to hear you're back.

Jennifer and Debbie were mean again today. Jennifer stole my diary and started ripping pages out. She tossed it to Debbie. They played "keep-away" by throwing it back and forth between them until I punched Debbie in the nose. I wish I hadn't.

Her parents filed a police report. I wasn't arrested, but I had to sit in the office with a cop and the temporary principal, Ms. Carter (our regular principal is on leave). Everyone blamed me. Seriously. They're so dumb. Jennifer started it. Debbie aided and abetted her. They aggravated me. I socked her one.

The cop made the report. When I left the office, I saw Debbie with her dad and another cop. Probably spreading lies. This was so stupid. I wanted to go home and hang out with you. Not deal with ego-tripping police and emotionally wounded idiot Jennifer. You're not complicated, Herk. You're so simple.

I couldn't find the pages torn from my diary. Maybe Jennifer kept them. I hate her.

October 22, 1992

Dear Herk,

There's a hitch in our step. I asked Mr. Reese for the generator today. He said "no." He also told me to stop spreading lies about him. He said he has a wife and kids, blah blah. I never told anything to anyone.

Something unusual happened today. A boy, Randy Archuleta, gave me the missing pages from my diary. Such a gentleman. Why can't the other kids be like him? I asked him if he'd read the missing pages. He said of course not, they weren't his to read.

October 23, 1992

Dear H,

Jennifer and Debbie left me alone today. What a relief. It's nice to not be constantly confronted every day at school. I don't think I'll be friends with them, but I also don't think I'll hate them forever. Mr. Reese let me take the Van de Graaff generator home.

I did some minor experiments on you with it. Not all your parts work the same. Like your hind legs kinda work and your muzzle twitches — but that seems to be it. I guess saltwater isn't the best for dead pugs.

October 24, 1992

H,

Man, this whole anatomy thing is complicated. You now officially have the insides of one of those pound pugs. I thought stitching a dress from grandma's pattern was hard! You don't know hard until you've sewn up the belly of a pug.

Randy didn't talk to me today. I dunno what's up with him. Like why give me my diary pages back and not want to talk to me?

October 25, 1992

Dear Herk,

You have a new tail!

October 26, 1992

New chest and back.

October 27, 1992

New forelegs. They're different col-
ors, but that's okay. You're a wondrous
mix of fawn and black pugs. Very
pretty. Distinct. Unique. Distinguished.
Such a badass. I love you.

October 28, 1992

So, um, Herk. You know that song
"If You Wanna Be Happy" by Jimmy

Soul? It talks about marrying an ugly woman to be happy. He mentions a woman's eyes not matching, but that woman is a better catch. That describes our relationship. Your eyes don't match now, but still you're my destiny. I also put half the brain of another pug in you. Just to see.

October 29, 1992

Dear Herk,

Today is JUICE DAY!!!!!! Not that weird guy on infomercials trying to convert everyone to drinking juice, but electricity! The real nectar of the gods. Wires from the generator to the cute little bolts in your neck. Zap! You were alive enough to walk. Then we danced. I put on Little Anthony & the Imperials' "Shimmy, Shimmy, Ko-Ko-Bop." I'm not really sure how to bop dance, but you moved so well.

I watched *Wayne's World*. Again. I bought it from Hastings. I couldn't see it at the theater. Too young. I rented it once from Hastings. And then a bunch of times. When Hastings started sell-ing used copies last month, I grabbed one. I laughed. I cried. I didn't hurl. I think you also laughed.

October 30, 1992

Dearest Herk,

Gosh people are so rude! That gargoyle Jennifer was at it again today. She asked me what I was going to be for Halloween. I said "Nothing. I'm too old to trick-or-treat." Her friend Debbie then said she was going as me. Jennifer laughed. The stupid Social Clique Mafia laughed. Everyone laughed. Even Mr. Reese. It was so humiliating. I hate them. I'm especially mad at Mr. Reese. He makes me so angry. He's such a hypocrite.

I cried into my pillow. You comforted me. I put the radio to the oldies station and covered my face with the pillow. You snuggled up next to me. We're back.

※ ※ ※

October 31, 1992

Dear Herk,

YOU ROCK! Man, today was a blast.
So much happened.

Most of the day was beyond boring.
When I was little, Mom used to play a
"Sounds of Halloween" record. I'm too
old for that. But I did listen to a Vincent Price record of hers today: *Tales
of Witches, Ghouls, and Goblins*. With
nobody else in the world to reassure
me, Mr. Price reassured me. It's amazing he's still alive. Guess who else is
alive today?

Dad asked why I wasn't carving any pumpkins for Halloween.

"This Halloween I don't carve pumpkins," I said. He just walked away with an amused look on his face. I didn't tell him what I planned to carve. He went to the store.

I knew Debbie lived on the east side of town. This part of town is a cesspit of McMansions in various shades of beige, the lamest color. The street sits on the other side of Highway 89. The people there probably give out gold-dusted candy corn to trick-or-treaters. I didn't feel like riding my bike there. I also didn't feel like asking someone for a ride. There was still the problem of the new Herk ... I mean you still look like a pug but a very, very special pug. I didn't want to E.T. you in some blanket.

There was a knock at our door after nightfall. Was it trick-or-treaters? I looked through the keyhole. The person looked strange. It was a person, but with exaggerated features. She held a plastic jack-o-lantern. I opened the door.

"Trick or treat!" she yelled. I could see what I was facing. She had the same eye color as me, but with snake eye contact lenses. She had the same hair color as me, but I could see the tell-tale strands of a wig. The bridge on her nose had been augmented with something. Putty? She wore Groucho

Marx-style eyebrows. She also seemed to have putty on her chin. She wore grunge-type clothes. The clothes had stains and patches and — I realized this was Debbie and she was really dressed up as me.

My heart sank. I opened my mouth to speak, but before I could even say anything she flung her pumpkin bucket at me. A green slime, like the one from Nickelodeon, flew out of the bucket and splashed me on my face. Some even got in my mouth. It tasted so gross. I wanted to cry. My eyes were already wet with slime. I heard girls laughing. I heard a low rumble.

The rumble came from behind me. A snort. A huff. It was you! My new

Herk! You charged so fast that you broke through the screen door. You bit Debbie on the leg and with a yank you broke it off mid-shin and spit the bloody stump out. You licked your mouth. I saw the determination in your mismatched eyes. Your head tilted in your quizzical way.

"Psycho dog! You gotta help me!" she yelled, crying like a baby and bleeding like the stuck pig she was. "I'm sorry," she said. "It was a prank."

"My dog doesn't like pranks," I said, trying to sound like a twelve-year-old girl version of Clint Eastwood.

Debbie flopped around our porch like a dying fish-pig.

"Don't let me bleed to death!" she begged.

"Oh, I won't," I said.

"Thank God!" she said.

"Sic 'em," I told you.

You were wonderful! You jumped onto Debbie and ripped her stupid Debbie throat from her stupid Debbie body. She tried to scream and couldn't. She tried to run and couldn't. She fell limp. You stood over her body, proud of your handiwork.

"Who's a good Herk?" I asked. I think I saw you smile.

Hey Deb," a voice said. "These people barely had any candy. Some old guy gave us apples. We're done trick-or- ... what is that?" I recognized the voice as Jennifer's. She had some of her Social Clique Mafia with her.

"Heavenly Father! What is that?" she asked. I saw Jennifer. She was dressed as a green witch. It certainly became her. She also carried a stupid broom with her.

"Is that thing a dog?" she asked.

"That's my Herk."

"It's almost as ugly as you are," she said. She laughed. You ran at her. She swung the broom at you. You bit it in half. She tried to poke you with the jagged handle, but she tripped and impaled herself on the bottom half. Blood gurgled up. She moaned "Lord." She staggered to her feet. You charged her again and bit her leg. This time you didn't break it in half. You ran back to me.

"Damn freak pug!" she screamed.

You dropped something in front of me on the porch. It was flesh, bone, and tendon. It was her kneecap. Cool.

"Now the other one, Herk," I said.

Sure enough, the diligent doggy Herk tore off her other kneecap and brought it to me.

"Please. Please. Please don't kill me," Jennifer begged.

"I won't," I said. I gave her a knowing look while you tore her to pieces, bit by bit, depositing the pieces of Jennifer on the porch.

It was funny. I was worried about getting into trouble, but when dad

came home, he mentioned the Halloween decorations were very realistic. He
brought some pumpkin cookies home
from the store. You even had one. You
ate the whole cookie in one bite! Today
was the perfect Halloween.

Author Inspiration

I first heard "Feed My Frankenstein" when I saw Wayne's World on video in 1992. Much like my story's protagonist, I grew up in Layton, Utah, had a ba- dass pug, and attended the traumatic Central Davis Junior High. Unlike her, I never resurrected any dead pugs. I had the idea for "Feed My Pugenstein" for nearly a decade before this anthol- ogy gave me the opportunity to turn my idea into a published story. I'm so happy to be included with all these other wonderful writers. To this date, the best concert I ever attended was an Alice Cooper concert at Saltair, near

the Great Salt Lake, my sister roped
me into.

"A Child Born of Ashes and Shattered Teeth"
by Michael Picco

You have to get the temperature just right. If it's off, even a little bit, you don't get that "flush of life."

I find that the optimum temperature for embalming fluid is between 104 and 106 degrees. Beyond 115 degrees, the fluid can scald you. Lower than 80, and the chemicals tend to gel and solidify. And they are so much more difficult to circulate at that temperature. It's taken me a good deal of trial and error to figure out what works and what doesn't. It's ongoing. A work in progress, if you like. I am thinking of installing heat lamps here in the preparation room, but I fear that may cause other issues, both with the clients and with my employer.

Maybe I should consider installing heating pads instead? After all, I could mount them under the prep tables—out of sight, out of mind, as they say. I could run the cords through the table legs and attach a power strip to the table's lower lip, all without drawing any undue attention. I know this may sound like a lot of trouble, but it's worth it.

And people say I'm lazy.

Most of what I see day-to-day are the elderly deceased, but the fatalities from disease come in a close second. Less prevalent are accidental deaths, but those tend to be riddled with physical trauma. All of these corpses tend to be less than optimal specimens for what I ultimately have in mind—and are better suited to experimentation than anything else. Testing on these kind of subjects leaves me better prepared for when an <u>ideal</u> specimen comes in. It's not an exact science—in fact, it's definitely more art than science, if I'm being frank. It's taken me <u>years</u> to finally figure out the correct embalming fluid formula and temperature combination; and months more to determine which combination leaves the orifices and limbs the most pliable. Never mind all of the additional precautions I need to take—so as not to get caught indulging my appetites.

Fortunately for me, the mortuary has had a lot of new clients lately. COVID-19 related deaths have nearly doubled my supply. While this particular variety of sex mannequin isn't ideal, they do provide a ready inventory of trial candidates. And, while the prospect of getting sick is <u>concerning</u>, it's not really a deterrent. After all, there are germicides that can be employed <u>in extremis</u>.

But I don't have to worry about *that* issue today.

This most recent arrival is nice and fresh, you see—a girl in her late teens. I'm told she was attending the University here in Arkham. Such a loss, right? Hah! Don't get me started! Her intake form indicates she died from a closed head injury—meaning there's no noticeable trauma to her body. She's what we in the industry call an "attended death" (that is, one that occurred while she was in a hospital setting). And that means no autopsy was necessary. And no autopsy means no autopsy incisions. That's key. It can be difficult to "perform" while staring down a large sutured wound. Maybe I am being too fastidious, but I like my fucklets ... well ... "pristine."

You can tell right away that this one is not from around here. She's not <u>local</u>, I mean. She's got those big city looks to her: piercings and tattoos in all kinds of strange places. She has a tiny trail of stars tattooed under her left breast (the pierced one), some filled in, some not, and some ink on her lower abdomen, just below her navel (some kind of strange sigil—Wiccan or something, I'd guess). She has a tramp stamp, too ... but it's gotten pretty lost in the bruising that's occurred postmortem. The blood pools in the lower parts of the body so quickly after death. The flesh around her heels, lower back and on the tips of her shoulders has turned yellowish-brown, bruising like the flesh of a rotten apple. But that's okay. The front of her looks just fine.

Face up and in the right light, she almost looks alive.

She had blue eyes, this one (for some reason, blue seems especially susceptible to the dull glazing that occurs after death). But that is easily remedied. All I have to do is rub a few drops of glycerin into her eyes to shine them up. I prefer that my lover's eyes remain open (again you know: for the "illusion of life"). Did you know the tissue around the iris can actually start to <u>wrinkle</u> if left untreated? That's why most morticians simply place a drop superglue under each eyelid prior to an open casket viewing. Not only does that keep the deceased's eyes closed, but it also seals the membrane, maintaining the moist "plumpness" of the eye.

Ah, the little things you learn in undertaker school!

This new arrival is pretty, too. "Picturesque," you might say. It may sound like a cheap pick-up line, but she seems oddly <u>familiar</u>, too. I feel as though I have seen her before ... I just can't remember where. She's cold, of course, but not just physically, I imagine. Even dead, she has that "frigid" look to her. You can just tell with girls like her. I've seen dozens of bitches like her in my life. They're the sort who grimace and squirm away from you at the slightest approach; their lips curled up in contempt; sneering and telling me I am too fat and dis-gusting to even speak to—only to de-base themselves with some scumbag later.

Yeah ... this one just gives off that sort of vibe: the one that says she was just too damn good for a man like me. Alive, I'm guessing she wouldn't have even <u>talked</u> to me, much less anything else. And if we had spoken, she would have just rolled her eyes at me then joked about it to all her little snobby university friends. She would have left me alone and broken, quickly dismissing all the shame she inflicted on me and others like me. She would have been oblivious to the fallout and loneliness and depression and hatred that engenders. Honey-dippers like her never have a clue.

I'm karmic payback for that kind of behavior. You say you don't want me, huh? How about <u>when you can't say no anymore</u>?

So, while you may consider her death a loss, I'm <u>glad</u> she's dead. Fewer stuck-up whores like her in the world is a good thing, if you ask me. And I am glad she found her way to me here. Like I said: it's karma. The diener who rolled her in must have caught me outright staring at her; but once I noticed her scrutiny, I managed to scowl and huff, muttering under my breath about what a shame it was that this poor girl was taken so early. Given the diener's look of disgust, I don't think my performance was all that believable, but she left without saying another word. I should be more careful, but it's rare I get a specimen as well-preserved and attractive as this one.

And admittedly, my desire is burning holes in my restraint at this point.

The funeral director won't be back here until after the weekend holiday, so that gives me plenty of time to enjoy her "second show." Quality time, you might call it, but I call it *sexy* time. I need to make certain the rest of the staff are gone before I get started though. That's one lesson I learned early on! A few years ago, one of the mortuary assistants nearly walked in on me with my pants down around my ankles. <u>En flagrante delicto</u>, as they say. I've since installed a latch bolt on the back of the preparation room door, so I can lock it when necessary. But really, after hours, people rarely venture down here. What happens in the mortuary, stays in the mortuary, I like to say.

Vegas has nothing on the parties I throw myself down here.

Foreplay consists of slowly unzipping the body bag—a slow-motion strip tease. Sometimes, I will even put on some beatnik jazz, heavy on the high hat, for effect, but not tonight. Tonight, I want to give this little whisker biscuit my undivided attention. As the bag settles around the body, I am engulfed in a plume of musty esters mixed with polyethylene; the fading hint of expired floral perfume; sweat and cigarette smoke. Revealing a body for the first time can be *so* arousing— especially when they've been sealed up a while. There's a raw meat kind of smell to the dead, but it's hard to describe if you're not used to it. I slip my thumb into her mouth as I strip off the bag, gauging the extent of morbidity from the condition of her tongue. It's still soft and pliable … but a little dry.

I take a sip of whisky from my hip flask and spit it into her mouth. I can hear it trickle and gurgle down her throat, and inexplicably, I catch a whiff of spent cinders. I lean in closer and rub my thumb over her lips. They're still remarkably soft, too. I gently bite her lower lip and taste the sec-ond-hand whiskey there mixed with a little blood. The skin breaks so easily after you die. My saliva mixes with her blood and the whiskey, smearing over her chin—and suddenly she looks ut-terly wanton … lascivious.

If I don't drain her right away, she's going to get pretty muddy-looking and stiff, especially on her anterior side. And that just won't do. Besides, I'm aching to get started. As I said before: the flush of life is pivotal to a realistic experience. Nothing kills a boner faster than a cold hole.

My name is Balian L'Ugurluer, but because nobody can pronounce my Turkish name, most people simply call me "BLU." Even my boss, the funeral director, calls me "Big BLU" behind my back. I overheard him say once that working in the morgue is the perfect job for me, because nobody ever has to see my fat ugly ass. <u>As if</u> I can help my alopecia, my chronic acne, my ticks and affectations, and my constant weight issues. I've tried! Oh, how I've tried! Creams and diets and scrubs and hypno-therapy … you name it! Bah! You know what? I am as god <u>made</u> me—and apparently, there is nothing I can do about it! If god has decreed that I must spend my days and nights down here, then so be it! I may be "alone," but I never have to be lonely. Here, in the bowels of the mortuary, I alleviate the curse god bestowed on me the only way I can. You may say I'm sick, but I would say I am <u>resourceful</u>.

The diener's look of disgust is just *so* typical. She thinks she's better than me! All of them do! They think I don't understand their slights; that I'm stupid because I grew up in Izmir; that because I am an immigrant, I have no understanding of their insults! But, I hear them. I know what they whisper behind my back. I know they taunt me. They call me "The Big Blu Turk" or "Igor the Incel": "<u>Igor</u>," *they'll say.* "<u>How on earth did you get so gross and fat? Pick up the pace, Igor! We haven't got all night, you creepy fuck! Hey, Stoopid—yeah you, Blu, you big, fat fuck—can't you do anything right?</u>" Oh, how they jeer and impersonate me, loping behind me like a hunchback, their mouths ajar and fat tongues lolling. How their hateful laughter burns and stings!

Humanity has never been humane, I suppose. I do the best I can, even though I get no credit for all my efforts. I wonder sometimes why I even try.

Perhaps they are right. Perhaps I don't <u>deserve</u> a good life. Perhaps I am unworthy of love. No ... I mustn't think that way. I am determined to embrace the fate god has imposed on me. I may be ugly, and I may be fat; but as I said, I am resourceful. More resourceful than any of them realize ... or even suspect. Maybe I seem "creepy," but none of them truly know me. Why should I feel guilty about what I do? After all, what possible crime is being committed here? I am making *love* after all! I'm not inflicting any trauma—physically or emotionally. At least, not the sort that matters. There are never any sneers, or rejections ... and most importantly, there are no refusals.

Let me ask you: how can you afford someone basic respect and dignity when you yourself have long been denied the same? I think I am entitled to a little compensation for my mistreatment. A little "sexual healing" at the end of a long day. Besides, I only indulge my fetish every now and then— hardly often enough to balance all the abuse and indignities I've received. To my way of thinking, I have demonstrated <u>remarkable</u> restraint. I've been very judicious; even <u>discerning</u> some might say.

It's all just a game, isn't it? Figuring out how to satisfy one's basic animal drives while mitigating my mistreatment—with the only resources I have available. Oh sure, I could solicit a prostitute or buy a sex doll, but why debase myself with one of those when I have so many opportunities presented to me here … for free?

Besides, you <u>have</u> to let the pressure off every now and then, or else you'll just go crazy … or get too <u>careless</u>. That's been my issue lately. I've gone too long between "girlfriends" I suppose. That incident with the diener is just another indication that I need to work on concealing my intentions. While I maintain that these little private exploits of mine are a <u>victimless</u> crime, I know that's a minority opinion. I know there would be consequences if I were to be caught. But, to be perfectly frank with you, the risk of getting caught makes it all the more exciting!

The last decent fuck-puppet came through here about three years ago. She wasn't anywhere near as good-looking as the blue-eyed specimen laid on my embalming table now, but she was fit and trim enough. She was married to a doctor and once surely considered a "trophy wife," but in death, without her fancy clothes and make-up, she was rendered so very, very ordinary. She had slit her wrists in the bath if I remember correctly, and I had a tough time averting my gaze from the bloody gashes on both of her wrists. But, since she arrived nearly bloodless, her postmortem bruising was almost nonexistent. You know what the best thing about her was though? Even in death, her tits were still nice and firm. Given the scars underneath both breasts, I suspect I had her silicone implants to thank for that. Natural tissue, especially fatty tissue, can become so easily damaged postmortem. Why, an are-ola can come right off in your hands if you're too rough with it.

Thankfully, I've found that silicone supports the surrounding tissue and makes it so much more durable. Which is good, because I do like it <u>rough</u>. The weird thing about that particular meat-doll—what made her so mem-orable … and so very, very fuckable—was that she <u>lactated</u> blood. Not a lot, mind you—just a dribble or so; but it was enough to instantly arouse me. I shudder now just thinking about it!

And that's when it hit me! The pea-nut smuggler on the table has the same icy blue eyes <u>as her mother</u>! I check the transfer manifest. Sure enough: the two women share the same last name! No wonder she seemed so familiar!

Now, I don't usually make it a point to attend a funeral service, much less be present when a client's remains are returned to a family member (or family members in this case: the husband and his teenage daughter). Not only does the boss not want me hanging around, but there are also more personal reasons why I avoid the client's family. I guess my main concern is that my carefully-crafted façade might slip, and the family might be able to somehow divine my more prurient interest in the deceased; or they might glimpse me struggling to stifle one of my troublesome nervous titters.

But, given my "exploits" with the doctor's late wife, I *had* to make an exception. I had one last thing to give them, you see. Before the cremation urn was sealed, I had surreptitiously seeded the woman's still smoldering ashes. How my worm vomit sizzled and hissed as I ejaculated over her re-mains! So then, at the funeral, as her daughter clutched her mother's urn to her bosom, I imagined my meat milk impregnating her ashes, gestating in the urn like a sepulchral womb—a child born of ashes and shattered teeth.

Shattered teeth, you ask? Yes ... the fires of cremation don't consume everything, only the softer tissues and smaller bones. Except for the teeth, that is. The teeth nearly always shatter during the cremation process. It has something to do with the enamel, I'm told. If you listen closely enough, you can hear the teeth pop and splinter during cremation; the fragments ricocheting off the insides of the crematorium. And, it's true: you never find whole teeth in the ashen remains. Only the broken pieces mixed in with the larger bones—the femurs, the skull, and the like (you know: the dense bones that have to be crushed and ground down afterwards—pulver-ized into more manageable chips).

Yeah ... the doctor's wife was taken from me too soon! Following the fu-neral, as the days turned to weeks, I found my thoughts returning to her more and more. I began to see her face everywhere! I couldn't concen-trate. I could barely sleep. Every cold breast I caressed, I thought of her. I tasted her coppery lactation at every meal. How often did I wish I could have had more time with her! Another chance to take her for the first time. Another chance to make her mine.

Her daughter is a little older now, but her resemblance to her mother is remarkable! I don't know why I didn't make the connection before, but I guess you could say I was a little distracted when we first "met." Knowing who she is only makes me want her more.

The level of difficulty removing the blood from the body is directly proportional to how long someone's been dead. As I mentioned before, once the blood begins to coagulate, it tends to settle and can lead to a sort of purple-black bruising in the low-lying sections of a body. The longer the body is left unattended, the more "bruised" looking the tissue becomes, and, the harder it becomes to adequately drain. Since Little Miss Blue-Eyes here was an "attended death," her postmortem bruising has been minimal. I suspect she was transferred to cold storage almost immediately after her life support was removed.

I make a tiny incision near the right collarbone, searching for the carotid artery and internal jugular vein. I insert the drainage hose, connect it to the embalmer, and start the pump. I thought I would need to use angled forceps to help facilitate blood flow, but after only a few clots, the blood sputters from the wound. Sometimes you have to increase the pressure on the embalmer to move the congealed blood from the corpse, but not for this one! No ... she's a bleeder!

I slip a foam block beneath her buttocks in order to allow for better drainage. As I lift her hips, she emits a subtle sigh. It's not uncommon for air to be trapped in the lungs after you die, vibrating the vocal cords in peculiar (dare I say, titillating ways). I caress her cold cheek and give it a good hard slap. "Quiet now, lover ..." I scold her as I lick her chilled and flattened nipple. Just for a moment, I see a thin, almost indiscernible column of smoke extend from the corner of her mouth. It dissipates almost as quickly as it appears. Again, I catch the reek of spent cigarettes.

Somewhere, deep in her bowels I can hear something gurgle.

I press my ear to her belly, just above her <u>mons pubis</u>, my fingers delighting in the downy peach fuzz curled there. My fingers absently brush the glyph tattooed just under her belly button. The area shouldn't be warm … but it is. <u>Isn't that odd?</u> Just a tiny ball of heat that seems to build as her blood sputters into the drain. It's almost as though the blood was keeping something down there from … <u>igniting</u>. Probably some exothermic microbial activity in the lower bowel. Strange … but you see some odd phenomena in the mortuary business.

Dying is hard; but death is brutal.

Once, I processed the corpse of a child who had been attacked by a boa constrictor. The little boy couldn't have been more than four or five when it happened. The boy was too big for the snake to fully devour, but he had the snake's teeth marks all over him. The boa had apparently been at it awhile, as there was no part of the child left unscathed. I've seen motorcycle accidents where the rider's legs have been literally been <u>shaved</u> off, left in a bloody smear over a quarter of a mile of rough pavement. And then there are the pitiful souls who die on the toilet. After death, blood settles quickly into the male genitalia. If left long enough, the testicles elongate and inevitably dip down into the basin. Immersed in the water, the tissue deteriorates quickly, and the rot travels up into the groin, eventually spreading to perineum. Once it takes root there, a man's entire lower digestive system can collapse <u>through the anus</u> and into the toilet!

It's just when I start to inject the embalming fluid (and take my pants down) that my love puppet emits a deep and sonorous belch. It's a long and horrible exhalation ... well beyond the capacity for human lungs to produce. <u>That</u> sort of thing is far less common an occurrence and one which repulses me immediately. That degree of intestinal gas build-up doesn't usually occur in someone so recently deceased. I decide to puncture the bowel in order to aspirate the remainder of it. I don't want her "emitting" during our time together.

Rather than pull my pants back up, I turn and shuffle over to my work tray. I am just about to select an appropriate trocar when I hear something behind me *snap*. I slowly pivot, watching in disbelief as a smoldering rib tears free of my lover's abdomen. Inexplicably, her stomach begins to blister and peel. My first thought is that I've turned the setting on the embalmer too high, and the chemicals have somehow started to combust inside her.

To my growing horror, I see something black like smoke—some kind
of thick vile cloud—begin to billow
out of her. The pall is thick, oily—and
very, very hot. Panicked, I stumble
backward. My feet become entangled
in my trousers and I end up tumbling
onto the floor. I hear my right arm
snap as try to catch myself and for
a moment, the room grows dim and
hazy. I am quickly revived by the
stench of scorched carrion, excrement,
and cinders. Smoke billows from the
girl's loins—not unlike some kind of
terrifying menstrual pyroclastic flow—
scorching and charring her tender
white thighs. Fat pops and sizzles as it
drizzles over the edge of the prepara-

tion table. As the searing cloud spills from the steel table and onto the floor, the linoleum peels away in twisted black ribbons.

I gape in terror as her head lolls off the block, and she appears to fix me with her dreadful gaze. Her mouth droops open, and from it issues a ghastly sigh that steadily builds to a howl. Her once beautiful blue eyes seem to corrode to a sickly reddish gray before the cornea itself ignites and collapses in on itself.

Her body grows steadily hotter, becoming nearly incandescent—a white-hot heat that scorches my exposed skin. I raise my hands to shield my face from the inexplicable conflagration, the nylon in my shirt melting onto my skin. Gasping and clutching my broken arm, I push myself against the door of the mortuary's walk-in freezer. The roar of the conflagration commingles with the girl's screams, merging into a protracted and dreadful howl that erodes my crumbling sanity. Her corpse disintegrates into a maelstrom of ashes and seething gas. The growing vortex draws ever closer to me even as I struggle to shield myself from the blaze.

It's then I see something begin to emerge from the frenzy. A gaunt and shadowy figure seems to extract itself from the ashes and charred bones. It's something ebon and sinewy. I hear

its bony fingers scrape along the insides of the girl's slender hip bones,
lifting itself free from her smoldering
womb. The unholy thing perches man-
tis-like atop the blackened prep table.
Crouching there among the embers
of her bones, it licks lumps of charred
flesh from its serrated forearms and
growls hungrily.

Author Inspiration

The story draws its inspiration from Alice Cooper's song "Blue Turk", which appears on his 1972 Album, <u>School's Out</u>. "A Child Born..." is what I call a "slow burn" ... that is, the story gets more and more bizarre and disturbing as it goes (which I feel is reflective of mood of "Blue Turk").

Besides, I love the beatnik appeal of this song—especially the jazzy base-line—and thought it might provide readers exposure to a lesser-known tune of Cooper's. I have tried to paint BLU as a typical incel, who justifies his misdeeds by the "mistreatment" he has received from women and from his co-workers at the mortuary. This is a story about his comeuppance and should resonate with readers who find the narrator, and what he does, so appalling.

Author Biographies

Ross Baxter

After thirty years of naval service, Ross Baxter now concentrates on writing short stories. He has won a number of awards, and had a story included on the 2017 HWA Bram Stoker reading list. Married to a Norwegian and with two Anglo-Viking kids, he now lives in Derby, England.

Website: https://rossbaxter.word-press.com/

Melissa Dudek

Melissa M. Dudek proudly hails from Poway, California, but has lived in Charlottesville, Virginia, for the last dozen years. By day, she is an assistant director of athletic communications for the Virginia Cavaliers. She writes about everything but sports in her free time. The author of three novels earned a master's degree in creative writing from the University of Edinburgh, graduating with distinction. When not writing, she is chasing birds and bears all over the planet and is a member of the #7ContinentClub. Follow her on Instagram @moweevil and X (f.k.a. Twitter) @dudekproblems.

Bert Edens

Bert is an author and editor who has always been one to read anything put in front of him, a passion he still enjoys, reading in all genres. Long ago, when text-based browsers still roamed the earth, he had many short pieces published on various webzines that no longer exist, covering genres from non-fiction to horror to sci-fi to erotica. He also had a story about his older son published in a collection of stories about premature babies.

Then life raising said older son, as well as the implied younger son, interceded, and he found little time to write. Now, as his sons are adults, he has begun finding more time to write.

He has recently been published in multiple anthologies of flash fiction as well as in a magazine dedicated to supporting children with special needs. He also has multiple non-fiction and fiction pieces accepted for future publication.

When not writing, he is active as a martial arts instructor, software developer, an amateur chef, and a strong proponent for disability rights and empowerment of women. You are just as likely to find him in front of a keyboard, on a martial arts mat, baking banana bread, or sitting cross-legged in a used bookstore soaking up the bibliophilic aroma and feeding his addiction for rare or unusual cookbooks.

He lives in Arkansas with Carrie, the wife he doesn't deserve; his older son, Zak; two Corgis who rightly believe they are royalty; and a lovable but spoiled brat of a toy poodle.

If you feel so inclined, drop him a note at bert@bert-edens.com.

Jason R Frei

Jason R Frei lives in Eastern Pennsylvania where he works as a therapist with children and adolescents. He writes speculative fiction culled from the experiences of his life and those he works with. He blends science fiction, fantasy, and horror into new creations. His fiction has appeared in anthologies by Pulse Publishing, Hellbound Books Publishing, Gravestone Press, Crimson Pinnacle Press, Phobica Books, and the Horror Writer's Association. Besides writing, Jason enjoys all things geeky, from comics to D&D to video games. Visit him online: https://facebook.com/odinstones

L.V. Gaudet

L. V. Gaudet is a Canadian author of dark fiction and member of, and volunteer with, the Manitoba Writers' Guild, and Horror Writers Association. In addition to more than 40 flash fiction, short stories, and book review publications over the years, Lori has

580

ten books published under two pen names and is the editor of <u>Beyond Boundaries</u> anthology, the Manitoba Writers' Guild's first Dave Williamson National Short Story Compilation. Lori's first published novel, <u>Where the Bodies Are</u>, was published by Second Wind Publishing in 2014, then again under the imprint Indigo Sea Press in 2016. Lori's biggest wish is to win a Bram Stoker award. Growing up with a love of the darker side of fiction, Lori has had, since reading that first novel, a passion for the idea of creating stories and worlds a person can get lost in.

Recent publications include short stories "Dark Shadows" published 2021

(Dragon Soul Press's <u>All Dark Places</u> *3* anthology) and "The Darkest Night" published 2022 (Dragon Soul Press's <u>Haunt</u> anthology).

You can follow L. V. Gaudet's sinister meanderings in a few favourite haunts:

Facebook Page: LVGaudet.Author: <u>https://www.facebook.com/LVGaudet.Author</u>

Instagram: lv_gaudet: <u>https://www.instagram.com/lv_gaudet/</u>

Threads: lv_gaudet: <u>https://www.threads.net/@lv_gaudet</u>

TikTok: @lv_gaudet: (sorry in advance for all the dog videos) <u>https://www.tiktok.com/@lv_gaudet</u>

Website: lvgaudet: <u>https://lvgaudet.wixsite.com/lvgaudet</u>

Fan blog: LV Gaudet, Author of Dark Fiction: https://lvgaudet.wordpress.com

Rambling author blog: The Intangible World of the Literary Mind: https://lvgwriting.wordpress.com

D.A. Latham

D.A. Latham is an Army brat, having grown up all over the United States and Germany. When her father retired in 1989, her family moved back to New England. She loves the beach, spending time in her backyard reading, and Fall. Writing has always been a passion of hers, and she has just recently started to get her works published. While she mostly reads horror, she loves books of any genre. She is co-host of the YouTube show, <u>What's in The Box: Episodes of Horror</u> and has been published in several anthologies, as well as having a series of extreme horror shorts she co-authored on Godless.

Shannon Lawrence

A fan of all things fantastical and frightening, Shannon Lawrence writes in her dungeon when her minions allow, often accompanied by her familiars. She writes primarily horror and fantasy. Her stories can be found in over fifty anthologies and magazines, and her four solo collections and non-fiction titles can be found in stores and online. You can also find her as a co-host of the podcast Mysteries, Monsters, & Mayhem. When she's not writing, she's hiking through the wilds of Colorado and photographing her magnificent surroundings. Though she often misses the Oregon coast, the majestic and rugged Rockies are a sight she could never part with. Besides, in Colorado there's always a place to hide a body or birth a monster. What more could she ask for?

Find her at:

thewarriormuse.com or mysteriesmonstersmayhem.com.

Paul Lubaczewski

Paul lived all over the country before settling in Appalachia over fifteen years ago with his wife Leslie and their son. He also has two adult children living in his native Pennsylvania. He is the author of six novels, two collections, and more on the way. Paul is a member of the Horror Writers Association, appearing on the panel for horror comedy at the 2021 Stoker Con. He has a dark and serious horror side, but he has also never answered the question "Is everything a joke with you?" correctly once in his entire life. All links can be found here https://linktr.ee/paullubaczewski.

D E McCluskey

Born in Liverpool in the UK, Dave McCluskey left school and began working in a music shop selling guitars and drums and playing in local bands around the Liverpool music scene. When he realised that fame, fortune, and rock god status was proving rather elusive, he went to university, leading to him wasting almost 30 years of his life messing around with computers.

He became a novelist later in life, having been an avid reader since he was a child. He writes as D E McCluskey, mostly in the genre of horror (mainstream, extreme, and comedy), although he has been known to dabble in thrillers, romance, science fiction, fantasy, and also children's books (written as Dave McCluskey).

He began his writing career creating comics and graphic novels, thinking they would be easier to write and sell than traditional novels (how wrong he was). He then made the switch into the media of novels and audiobooks and has not looked back since.

His books include the highly regarded The Boyfriend, The Twelve, Cravings, Zola, and the historical thriller In The Mood for Murder.

Dave remains an avid football fan, although sometimes he wonders why, and he has been known to lurk around the stand-up comedy circuit in the North-West of England.

He lives at home with his partner, their two children, and a sausage dog with his own future children's book series, called Ted (Lord Teddington of Netherton).

Madison McSweeney

Madison McSweeney is a horror and dark fantasy writer from Ottawa, Ontario. She is the author of <u>The Forest Dreams with Teeth</u> (Demain Publishing), <u>The Doom That Came</u>

to Mellonville (Filthy Loot), and the poetry collection Fringewood (Alien Buddha Press). Her short fiction has appeared in anthologies like Zombie Punks, Fuck Off (Weirdpunk/ CLASH) Nightmare Sky: Stories of Astronomical Horror (Death Knell Press), and American Gothic Short Stories (Flame Tree).

Michael Picco

Michael Picco's work has been described as "gripping and deliciously disturbing," "full of foreboding and malicious intent," and "adaptive and exceptional." One editor says: "[Picco] conducts his nightmares with something between feverish grace and clammy ease." He is known for his use of visceral imagery, which, when combined with atmospheric settings, produce tales that endure—lingering with readers long past the telling.

Folklore, parasitic morphology, and theology are recurring motifs in his work. Scripture and classical literary references often form the ideological basis for a majority of his narratives. Folklore and regional cryptids feature prominently—with the intention of exposing readers to the lesser-known horrors that prowl the forsaken and abandoned corners of the world. Picco's nuanced approach to horror creates a sense of growing unease and tension that has helped to establish him as a distinctive voice in the genre.

Picco received his B.A. in English from Western State College in Colorado. He is a member of the Denver Horror Collective and the Colorado Independent Publishers Association. He is currently working on These Wretched Bones, a revision and expansion of some of his most popular published works. Find him at: www.michaelpicco.com.

Joe Scipione

Joe Scipione lives in the suburbs of Chicago with his wife and two kids. He is the author of Mr. Nightmare, The

Life and Times of Edward Morgan, Zoo: Eight Tales of Animal Horror, Decay, and Perhaps She Will Die. He has had short stories featured in numerous anthologies. He is a member of the Horror Writers Association. When he's not reading or writing you can usually find him cheering on one of the Boston sports teams or walking around the lakes near his home with his dog. Find him on Twitter/X or Instagram: @joescipione or at www.joescipione.com.

Petina Strohmer

Petina Strohmer is a traditionally published novelist who has also had eighteen (mainly horror) short stories published over the last two years. She lives in the magical Welsh mountains with a raggle-taggle assortment of rescued animals. For more information:

Email: petinastrohmer@gmail.com

Website: www.petinastrohmer.com.

Bryan Stubbles

Bryan is currently a caretaker to his elderly parents. He's published short nonfiction in Timber Ghost Press' <u>Out of Time</u>, short horror fiction in <u>Wasatch Witches</u> and <u>Six Guns Straight from Hell</u>, among others. His stage plays have been produced in three countries. He translates Korean

and Indonesian into English. His translations have been published in <u>Asymp-</u>
<u>tote</u> and <u>The Mercurian</u>, among others.
A dead country singer, Charlie Daniels,
blocked him on Twitter/X. Feel free to
follow him there: <u>http://www.twitter.</u>
<u>com/BStubbles</u>.

Bernardo Villela

Bernardo Villela has had short
fiction included in periodicals
such as <u>LatineLit</u>, <u>Penumbra On-</u>
<u>line</u>, and <u>Horror Tree</u>, plus in anthol-
ogies such as <u>We Deserve to Exist</u>,
<u>Enchanted Entrapments</u>, and <u>There's</u>
<u>More of Us Than You Know</u>. He's had
original poetry published by <u>Phan-</u>

tom Kangaroo, Straylight, and Raven's Quoth Press and translations published by AzonaL and Red Fern Review. You can find some of his other works here: https://linktr.ee/bernardovillela.

Milton Keynes UK
Ingram Content Group UK Ltd.
UKHW040801010224
437095UK00004B/245